YEAR ZERO

KEITH TAYLOR

Copyright © 2019 by Keith Taylor
All rights reserved. This book or any portion thereof
may not be reproduced or used in any manner whatsoever
without the express written permission of the publisher
except for the use of brief quotations in a book review.
First Printing, 2019

CHAPTER ONE
THIS PLACE IS A GRAVEYARD

YOU'RE STANDING IN the open air.

You can feel the sun warm your skin, its rich golden glow unbroken by cloud, and you dig your toes into the soft loam beneath your feet. A gentle breeze plays through your hair, a soothing breath of fresh, clean air that carries with it the sweet, invigorating tang of ripe mandarin oranges. All around you can hear the susurrus of dancing trees, the rustle of leaves waving in the breeze, and for a moment you simply stand where you are, entirely at peace, wishing this moment could go on forever.

After the horrors of San Francisco this feeling is beyond idyllic. The memories of the city's ruins are still fresh in your mind, the sights and smells razor sharp. You can still feel the dust burning your skin. The stale, scorched air of the impact crater. The stench of death and the choking shroud of ash clinging to every surface, suffocating you, strangling the life from everything in sight, so fresh and vivid it's as if you were still there. As if you were still standing in that bleak cemetery, haunted by the howling screams and frantic prayers of the dying.

As you stood amongst the bleached bones of the city you never imagined you'd see life again. You never imagined you might feel joy or peace, or even a fresh breeze on your skin. But now…

You open your eyes.

Now you see you're standing in the midst of a lush orange grove. You take a deep draft of the citrus-edged air and look around at the long, ordered lines of neatly manicured mandarin trees that stretch out in all directions, their tops arched above you to create a labyrinth of shaded tunnels. It's cool down here. The bright sunlight dapples the ground beneath the branches, and but for the breeze playing through the trees and the slow, steady rhythm of your breath the world is silent and still.

You rise up, leaving the sweet tang of the air

behind, and above the treetops the distant edge of the grove comes into view. Beyond the trees, all around you, verdant farmland stretches out flat to the horizon in an unbroken sea of brown, green and orange. It's *beautiful.* It's a landscape that seems to breathe life and hope back into the world. As you look around, though, you notice that something seems to be missing from this peaceful, entrancing Constable watercolor of a world: there are no people here.

The villages that cluster tightly between broad fields are deserted. Doors hang open, resting wide on their hinges as if the occupants didn't just forget to close them but didn't care. Farmhouses are empty, the crops untended, and the narrow roads that reach in ordered lines across this rural idyll are silent.

It takes no great insight to guess what happened here. As soon as you notice something amiss it seems obvious. The image shifts, a silhouette of a vase that suddenly becomes two faces, and once you've seen it it can't be unseen. It was there all along.

Now... now you can sense the fear still hanging in the air, a terror so sharp, so vivid that it seems to have burned itself on the atmosphere like the afterglow that hangs on the screen of an old TV long after the picture flickers out. In your mind's eye you can see what happened here so clearly you could be watching in real time.

Yesterday, just as the sun was beginning to set in the west, the people who called this place home saw two new suns rise in the south. Without warning twin stars exploded into life on the distant horizon, so bright that anyone who dared sneak a look was left blinking away the painful afterglow at best, flash blinded at worst, and as the dazzling brightness began to fade it was replaced by something these people had always feared, yet never expected to see beyond movie screens and their darkest nightmares.

They saw twin mushroom clouds blossom from the glow, billowing silently skyward in black, orange and red.

Most of them ran without a second thought. They piled into cars and trucks and raced further inland as fast as they could, desperate to stay ahead of the crowds they knew would soon choke up the roads. Some moved so quickly that they were already on the road before the blinding light had completely faded.

They didn't pack. Didn't have *time* to pack. They left with nothing but the clothes on their backs and watched the spectacle through their rear view mirrors, not sparing a moment's thought to where they were going. They thought only of what they were escaping. *To* didn't matter when *from* was so terrifying.

But some… some didn't run. Some stayed behind and watched, entranced and awestruck.

If you asked them they couldn't tell you why they didn't turn and run right away. They couldn't explain why they waited until the blinding flash had faded then stood and stared as the radioactive plumes climbed high into the atmosphere above San Francisco and Sacramento. They'd fear you wouldn't understand if they gave voice to their thoughts. They'd fear you'd think them heartless, cruel voyeurs to the apocalypse if they gave you the real reason they didn't turn and run with everyone else.

The truth was that they watched because it was *beautiful*. They watched because it was stunningly, heartrendingly captivating, a sight so terrible it *demanded* an audience. They couldn't tear their eyes away from a display of such power, violence and brutality, all of it played out in absolute silence.

The sound of the explosions didn't carry this far, at least not at first. The deafening roar lagged far behind the light, so they watched in frozen awe as San Francisco and Sacramento were silently erased from the earth. Open mouthed they watched as two great cities were reduced to rubble, and through tear filled eyes they witnessed their remains rise to the heavens.

By the time the expanding twin shock waves reached them they were little more than a light breeze, as soft as a lover's kiss, but when they finally hit it was enough to break the spell among the people who stayed to watch. The gust rocked them back on their feet, and it brought with it the stench of death.

Before the shock wave reached them these people had existed in a peaceful world, a world in which life flourished and grew, but when that soft, stale breath passed by they felt as if that expanding bubble had encapsulated them, drawn them in and imprisoned them in a new and darker world, this one hostile to life and light. Hostile to hope and joy.

That's when they started to run.

Most wouldn't be able to articulate why if you asked, but as soon as they felt that shock wave pass every last one of them turned and ran as one, with a single purpose. It wasn't to escape the fallout. It wasn't to stay ahead of the evacuating hordes. It wasn't even out of fear that another blast might be coming their way, closer to home.

No, they ran because each and every one of them

felt the desperate need to escape the bleak, hopeless bubble that was even now expanding away from them at the speed of sound. They wanted – *needed*, at a primal, visceral level – to get back to the other side of that shock wave, back into the world they'd known just moments ago, even though deep down they already knew that the explosions had eradicated that world forever. They knew there was no going back no matter how fast they ran, but it didn't keep them from trying.

You look down at the deserted orange grove spread out beneath you, and now you see it for what it is.

This place is a graveyard. It may have escaped the ravages of the nuclear blast, but just like San Francisco before it it's still tainted by death. These ripe mandarins will never be plucked from the trees. They'll fall and rot where they land. By the time anyone dares return to this place it will have been reclaimed by wilderness. The manicured trees and trimmed, uniform crops will have grown out like unkempt hair, spilling over boundaries, swallowing roads and blanketing villages and towns. By the time the people return this will once again be the Wild West.

But for now…

You turn to face an unexpected sound, a low rumble that seems to drift elusively on the breeze. *Is that an engine?*

You scan your eyes across the haunted landscape, searching for movement, and finally you catch the glistening reflection of sunlight in the distance, a mirror flash on a black ribbon. A silver car barrels down an empty, arrow straight country route, racing at a dangerous speed. It looks like it's barely staying on the road, kicking up wild rooster tails every time it veers onto the dusty shoulder.

Wait.

You move closer, and now you see it. A half mile ahead of the car is a truck, an indistinct smudge almost lost in the heat haze, and you watch as it turns and pulls to a stop in the middle of the road, its air brakes hissing, the radiating heat of its engine searing air that's already baked by the sun. A few figures climb down to the sun baked asphalt. Soldiers in uniform, all of them armed. You move in closer still, curious, and as you draw near you see the figures take up position in readiness for the approaching car.

Even closer, and now you're amongst the soldiers. You can feel their tension as they watch the car approach. Clipped, terse orders fly back and forth as rifles are nestled against shoulders, safeties are flipped off and fingers hover over triggers. Still the car shows no signs of slowing. No way to know if the driver has even *noticed* the looming roadblock ahead.

Now the car moves close enough that you can see the face of the driver. He *has* seen the truck. All three men in the car stare straight ahead, terrified, wide eyed and yelling, but the driver only steps harder on the gas and the car surges forward. A flicker of his eyes telegraphs his intentions. He's going to try to drive around the roadblock, veer onto the shoulder and skid across the loose surface until he's cleared the truck. You can see his hands grip the wheel tighter, his knuckles white as he prepares to turn.

And then the order goes up, and the soldiers open fire.

It all happens too quickly to be certain, but you'd swear you see surprise on the face of the driver a moment before the windshield shatters beneath a barrage of 7.62mm bullets. The car wildly fishtails as the front tires burst, and the engine sputters and dies as a line of holes punch through the hood.

Just a few seconds after the first shot the soldiers cease fire, and before the car even rolls to a stop the men begin to approach, carefully surrounding it, their weapons still drawn. They pull open the driver's door as the car comes to rest at the side of the road, and with swift military efficiency they reach in and check the bodies, search for weapons and rifle through the glove compartment, seat pockets and trunk. When they're satisfied the threat has been neutralized they turn back to the truck, walking almost casually, as if killing three men in cold blood was no big deal. Just another duty.

Now the truck roars back to life. The driver shifts into gear and swings it around in a wide arc, turning back the way it came, and as he squeezes the gas he waves a hand towards the field beside the road. At first it seems empty, but as you look closer you see an answering wave rise from what looks like a few tufts of dried grass.

It's a sentry, hidden in camouflage that blends perfectly with the tall grass around him. As the truck powers off down the road he settles in place once again, stock still, a rifle scope raised to his eye, and he patiently watches the road for anything that might approach.

•▼•

CHAPTER TWO
NO BALL KICKING, OK?

WE DID THIS to ourselves.

Those were the last words Valerie had spoken. The last thing she'd managed to say before the soldiers hauled her down from the truck, slipped a black bag over her head and dragged her out of sight, yelling and cursing until her voice faded into the distance.

Before Karen had time to even *begin* to process what she meant they'd returned for her, and by then she had bigger fish to fry. As they climbed into the back of the truck she begged them not to separate her from Emily. She pleaded with them, her words blending together into an unintelligible mess choked by tears, but they didn't respond. They didn't even seem to have heard her. The soldiers didn't show so much as a flicker of emotion as they dragged Karen away from her daughter, leaving her alone, scared and confused, crying for her mom with her hands bound painfully behind her back.

Emily didn't understand what was happening. She didn't know why the soldiers were taking her mom away and leaving her behind. She was *terrified*, and at the sight of her daughter's tears Karen had felt her momma bear instincts kick in. She'd screamed herself hoarse, kicking out wildly at her captors. She'd tried to close her teeth over any arm that came within biting distance. She'd kicked out at every uniform, and she'd yelled spit-flecked threats until someone out of sight finally lost patience with the performance.

The last thing she'd heard was a stern voice giving the order to shut her up. The last thing she'd *felt* was the butt of a rifle hitting her in the head for the second time in an hour, and after that… nothing. She hadn't passed out, thankfully, but the blow had been more than enough to send her tumbling to the ground like a puppet with cut strings.

Once that butt slammed into her head she could carry on yelling about as easily as she could sprout wings and fly away. It took every last ounce of fight out of her. Her vision had filled with sparking white lights, and as they dragged her away by her arms she'd watched, unable to move a muscle, as a soldier lifted Emily over his shoulder and carried her down from the truck kicking and screaming.

She'd wanted to drag herself to her feet and run back to grab her from him, but her limbs just wouldn't respond to her commands. She couldn't so much as wiggle her toes until long after they'd dumped her in this room, cuffed her hands to the back of a chair and locked the door behind her.

We did this to ourselves.

Karen repeated the words for the millionth time as she stared at the white, featureless wall of her... cell? *Is this a cell?* It damned sure looked like one. The steel chair firmly bolted to the floor was the only scrap of furniture. The floor and walls were painted flat white, and on the fourth wall – visible only if she twisted painfully in her chair – a pane of mirrored glass ran the length of the room. Aside from an angry cop and a table for him to slam with his fist it looked like every police interview room she'd ever seen on TV.

What had Valerie meant?

Karen played the words out in her head yet again,

as if the million and first time might be the charm, but she couldn't seem to think clearly. Everything felt… floaty, as if she were working on her second bottle of wine and could already hear the hangover whispering threats of tomorrow. The tender, swollen knot of flesh on the back of her head throbbed just as painfully as the lump on her brow, and with a sinking feeling she realized she probably had a concussion. The second in as many days.

Jesus. That can't be good for me.

There was no way of knowing how long she'd been locked in the room. Could have been hours. Could have been just minutes, but time didn't seem to pass in the empty cell. It wasn't just that there was no clock on the wall, but that the walls themselves seemed to *absorb* time. The flat, featureless white seemed designed to muffle and soften her perception, purpose built to turn her mind to soup. Karen could feel as if ten minutes had crawled by before realizing she'd only taken a half dozen breaths.

"OK, get it together, Karen," she whispered to herself in a scolding voice, feeling a cold sweat prick at her brow. "You have to stay strong for Emily."

She started to sing out loud, trying to distract herself from the eerie, suffocating silence, but she quickly fell silent when the sound of her voice echoed back to her in a minor key. The song left her mouth as a soothing lullaby, something she used to sing to Robbie while he was teething, but it was a stranger's voice that came back, a bleak funereal dirge bouncing off walls that seemed to be closing in on her inch by creeping inch.

By the time she finally heard a key turn in the lock she'd almost convinced herself that her sanity was slipping away. She was almost certain the sound was in her head until she saw the door begin to open, and that's when the fear kicked in. She nervously gripped the chair and planted her feet wide on the ground, bracing herself for whatever was about to happen. She felt her heart begin to race in her chest, and deep down she was sure she'd never leave this room alive. Not after seeing what they'd done to the men in the Prius. Not after hearing Valerie's warning.

The temperature in the room seemed to drop by a few degrees as a man entered, looming almost as tall as the doorway, his expression one of pure malevolence. He was a soldier, tall and well built, a sidearm strapped to his hip, and it was only when Karen noticed the swollen bruise burning at his cheek that she realized she recognized him. He'd been one of the men who dragged her from the truck, and now she got a good look at him the memories came flooding back. She'd caught him full in the face with a wild kick as he lowered her to the ground. No wonder he looked so mad.

"What do you want?" she demanded, trying and failing to hide the fear in her voice. She scolded herself for allowing it to tremble. "You can't keep me locked up in here! I've done nothing wrong!"

The soldier remained silent. He glowered at her as he held open the door, and behind him another man shuffled through before the soldier vanished, pulling the door closed behind him. The new arrival entered the room clumsily, dragging a black folding chair in one hand and juggling a mug of coffee and a sheaf of papers in the other. He flinched slightly as he heard the lock click behind him.

Karen's first reaction was surprise, followed by relief. All she'd seen here so far were men in uniform, tough and – she felt the throbbing pain in her head – decidedly aggressive, but this man was… well, he appeared to be the polar opposite. He was middle aged and running to chubby, his tan corduroy blazer hanging open to allow for the slight paunch that hung over his belt. He wore a pair of round horn-rimmed glasses that might have looked stylish on a younger, more attractive man, but resting on his face they gave him the air of a lecturer at a low rent community college.

The most arresting thing about him, though, was his hair. He was balding, but if there was a way to lose hair gracefully this man had chosen the path furthest from it. What little remained of his curly thatch was cut in such a way that it looked as if the top of his head had simply grown vertically through a full head of hair, a shiny, sweaty dome rising above a wispy ring of brown.

"Sorry for the… oh, damn," he mumbled as he tried to jiggle open the folding chair, tipping his mug and splashing his coffee on the floor at Karen's feet. "Would you mind holding this for a second?" He held out the dripping mug, and then noticed the handcuffs that bound her hands to the chair. "Oh, right, sorry. Umm…" Absently he glanced over to the mirrored glass at the back wall and called out. "Are the cuffs really necessary, do you think?"

As he waited for a response he finally managed to shake open his chair, the legs screeching across the floor, and with a graceless slump he lowered himself to the seat and shook his sheaf of paper, flicking away a little coffee that had spilled on it.

"Seriously, you guys? Is it OK if I…?" He waved at Karen's hands. "Sorry about this. Military types, y'know? They like to do things by the book."

Again he stared impatiently at the glass, and when he heard nothing but silence he hauled himself back to his feet with a sigh, clomped over to the window, cupped his hands and pressed his nose against the glass.

"Hello? Anyone there? Hello-*ooo*?"

After a long moment of silence he turned back to face Karen with an awkward smile. "Huh. I don't think anyone's in there," he said, stepping over to the chair and lowering himself into a crouch as he fished a key from his jacket pocket. "You always just assume, right? To be honest I feel a little cheated," he muttered, half to himself. "First time in a room with mirrored glass and there isn't even anyone on the other side."

He paused, staying his hand as he gripped the key in the lock. "Hey, you're not gonna try to escape or anything, right? I mean, there's nowhere to go. You wouldn't make it ten steps past the door before the guard put you on the ground, but I don't want to look like an idiot for uncuffing you, know what I mean? Can I trust you not to do anything crazy?"

"I'm not going anywhere without my daughter," Karen managed to reply. Her words slurred a little, and her tongue felt numb in her mouth. "Where's Emily? What have you done with her?"

With a click the cuffs came loose, and her hands were finally free for the first time since she'd been captured. She swung them out ahead of her, stretching out her aching, bloodless arms as the man returned to his chair, defensively shuffling it back a few inches out of her reach.

"Your daughter?" he asked, peering down at his papers as if he'd find the answer there. "Oh, don't worry, she's right as rain. She's in the mess right now eating her body weight in ice cream. She's a real sweetie, that one," he said, with a distracted smile that slowly faded as he studied his papers. He flipped the pages, frowning at the handwritten scrawl, and after a few moments of silence he looked up at Karen as if he'd forgotten she was there.

"So…" he said, squaring off the pages against his knee, "why don't you tell me what you were doing trespassing on a US Air Force base? Not the smartest of moves, given the events of the last couple of days."

"We weren't trespassing," Karen replied, her voice

still a little slurred and her mind working at half speed. Her fingers tingled with pins and needles. "We were looking for help. Someone stole my car. We were just trying to get to somewhere safe."

"Your car? You mean the Prius?" The man frowned and looked down at the front sheet. "Is your name Toby Zimmerman?"

"What? No, I'm Karen Keane."

"I see. And are you traveling with anyone named Toby Zimmerman? Perhaps the African American woman you were with? Or maybe the Hispanic gentleman?" He flashed her a smile. "Your daughter isn't Toby Zimmerman, is she?"

Karen frowned, confused. "What are you talking about?"

"Forgive me," he smiled, "'but I'm a bit of a stickler for details." He held up his hands. "Guilty as charged, your honor. It's just that the registration documents for that car tell us that it belongs to a Mr. Toby Zimmerman of Forest Hill, San Francisco. Now I know that none of you guys are Mr. Zimmerman, and the three young gentlemen who were caught in the deeply regrettable incident out on the road weren't carrying ID that would suggest any of them were of the... ah, the Zimmerman persuasion. So I guess I'm just wondering in what sense this was *your* car. Can you help me out?"

For a moment Karen could do nothing but stare at him, open mouthed. Maybe the whack on the head had been harder than she'd realized. She just couldn't understand why he…

"Sorry, are you *really* making a big deal about a stolen car when nukes are exploding across the country?"

The man let out a soft chuckle and shook his head. "Not at all, Ms. Keane. To be honest I don't care if you stole the Space Shuttle and took it on a joyride, but I'm just trying to get your story straight. I'm trying to figure out how and why we found you strolling toward an Air Force base at the highest level of alert in the aftermath of a nuclear attack. You tell me someone stole your car, but now it turns out that you *yourself* stole the car. I'm sure you can understand why I'm a little skeptical of your story when the first words out of your mouth were a lie."

Karen took a few seconds to gather her thoughts. Her mind was still just a little too foggy to understand what was really going on, but she got the sense that the sweaty, awkward man sitting in front of her wouldn't let up until he'd worn her down with a million questions. Everything about his demeanor screamed *lawyer*, and right now she just didn't have the energy for it.

"You want to get my story straight?" she asked, taking a deep breath. "OK, fine, let's get it straight."

For the next five minutes she spoke almost without pausing for breath. She fought through the confusion and ignored the throbbing pain in her head to tell the story of every last thing that had happened since the car accident on the highway the previous morning. She told him about the first car they'd stolen, the Corvette in the underground parking lot near the hospital. She told him about the looters in Union Square, and the collapse of the bay bridge. The struggle to turn off the ventilation fans, and the terror of finding Jared clutching onto her little girl in the control room. The radiation poisoning, stealing the Prius on the highway, and the dying couple in the pharmacy. She told him everything up until the point the truck has chased them across the field, and by the end of it all her vision swam behind the exhausted, frustrated tears in her eyes.

"Is that straight enough for you?" she demanded. "Or do you have any more dumbass questions?"

For a long moment the man stared silently at her, either carefully observing her or just shellshocked from the five minute long stream of consciousness rambling from an exhausted, mildly concussed woman, but eventually he pushed himself out of his chair and nodded toward the mirrored glass on the wall behind her.

"Story checks out," he said, as Karen spun around and narrowed her eyes at the window. "It's pretty much what we heard from the others, and unless they coached the kid I can't imagine they're involved. I recommend we cut them loose."

A few seconds later a scratchy voice rang out from a small speaker hanging from the ceiling above the window. "She's free to go."

Karen turned in her chair. "There was someone back there?" she asked, pointing at the window.

The man raised his hand to his mouth with a mock guilty expression. "Oops, you got me." He reached out a hand and waited for Karen to take it, helping her out of her chair. "Nobody gets interviewed without a witness. Base policy. And sorry about giving you the third degree. We just needed to figure out if you were with us or them. I'm Ted, by the way. Ted Krasinski. It's a pleasure to meet you."

"Them?" Karen felt like she was experiencing this conversation on a tape delay. She had no clue what the hell was going on. "Who's *them*?"

Krasinski raised an eyebrow. "You know… *them*. The people who did this. I'm sure you can understand why we're a little antsy about letting people just wander in off the street."

Karen felt her frustration finally reach breaking point. She tugged her hand from Ted's and snapped. "OK, look. If one more person gives me some cryptic bullshit about what's going on I'm going to start kicking people in the balls. Now would you please tell me what's happening here? Who attacked us? Just give it to me straight, OK?"

Krasinski looked flustered, and before he replied he surreptitiously turned away from Karen, protecting his crotch from possible attack. "OK," he said, trying for a soothing tone. "I can debrief you, no problem at all." He looked down at his mug, finding it almost empty. "Look, I need some fresh coffee, so how about we go grab some in the mess? You can see your little girl and your friends, and I'll try to answer any questions you have."

"*Fine*," Karen snapped, pointing to the door. "Lead the way."

Krasinski hustled over to the door and gave it three sharp raps, and a moment later it swung open to reveal the same soldier guarding it. He stepped aside as Krasinski led Karen out into the hallway, and the chubby man's cheeks glowed red as he turned back to her.

"Just make me a promise. No ball kicking, OK?"

CHAPTER THREE
ALL THE WAY DOWN HERE

THE MESS HALL resembled nothing so much as a vast, repurposed high school gymnasium. Rows of tables filled the space from wall to wall, each of them illuminated by the harsh fluorescent glow of strip lighting to supplement the dingy sunlight that crept in through the high, dusty windows.

The room seemed large enough to seat at least a thousand base staff at a time, but as Karen entered beside Krasinski she found it virtually deserted. Only a handful of the tables were occupied, and the only sounds were the sneaker squeaks of the cleaning staff as they shuffled across the rolled vinyl floor from table to table.

She scanned her eyes around the room, searching

for Emily in the sea of tables, and at first she didn't spot her. The little girl was sitting alone at a table in the middle of the mess, a sticky spoon in one hand and a squeeze bottle of chocolate sauce in the other, but she was almost completely hidden behind the industrial sized tub of vanilla ice cream that sat on the table before her.

Karen rushed across the room and swept her daughter up in a bear hug, tears pricking at her eyes as she joyfully held her. She barely even noticed that she'd managed to get more ice cream on her hands and face than in her mouth, and she didn't care that Emily was leaving sticky stains on her clothes.

"Oh, I'm so glad to see you," she cried. "Are you OK? Did anyone hurt you?" She leaned back and started to check Emily for signs of injury.

"Nuh uh. They just kept asking questions, and then they said I could eat all the ice cream I wanted if I stopped crying." She tried to wriggle from Karen's grip. "Mommy, don't squeeze me so tight. My tummy hurts."

"Sorry pumpkin," Karen laughed, carefully lowering the digestive time bomb to the ground. "I'm just so relieved you're OK. I couldn't stop worrying about you."

As Karen fussed over her daughter Valerie and Ramos entered the mess, closely followed by a young soldier who seemed to be apologizing profusely as he hurried after them. Karen turned at the sound of a hissed curse word and the echoed scrape of a chair kicked across the floor, and immediately it was clear that something had happened. Valerie looked furious, storming away from the young soldier at a fast walk, and the soldier's cheek glowed pink with a fresh hand print. Still he apologized, but it didn't look like Valerie was in any mood to accept it.

Ramos flashed Karen an awkward smile as he reached the table and grabbed a chair, and she gave him a questioning look. "What happened to— "

Ramos cut her off with an urgent wave of his hand an expression that said *Leave it alone.*

"If you'd like, ma'am, we can arrange for a hot shower," the soldier babbled, pulling a chair back for Valerie. "And I can find you some fresh towels and clean clothes." He seemed desperate for her approval, but it was clearly a fool's errand. Whatever he'd done to her he'd made an enemy for life.

Valerie shot him a look that could have burned a hole through an inch of solid steel. "I'm fine," she hissed, somehow managing to make those two words sound like a vicious rebuke. She ignored the chair he'd pulled out and took her own on the other side of the table. "You can get out of my sight now."

"Actually," Ramos said, meekly raising a hand, "it might not be a bad idea to get Emily cleaned up sooner rather than later. I want to make sure she doesn't still have any fallout in her hair. Better safe than sorry, right?" He looked up at the soldier. "Can you show her to the showers?"

"Yes, sir," the young man replied enthusiastically, eager to win favor. He held out a hand for Emily. "You want to come with me?"

Emily looked at Karen, who nodded, and she planted her spoon in the ice cream like a flag. "I guess so. I don't think I can eat any more anyway," she said, pushing the tub across the table, but a moment later seemed to have a change of heart. "Mommy, don't let them take the ice cream away, OK? I might be hungry again when I get back."

"If you say so, pumpkin," Karen skeptically smiled. By the look of the tub it would be weeks before she'd be able to face ice cream again.

Emily took another step away from the tub, wavered for a moment, and then grabbed the spoon for a final scoop. "OK, I'm ready now," she said, ice cream running down her chin as she offered the soldier her sticky hand. "Don't eat my ice cream, mommy."

"OK," agreed Karen. "We're just going to have a little grownup talk with this man." She pointed to Krasinski. "It'll still be here when you get back."

Emily nodded, satisfied that her treasure was safe, and finally she allowed the young soldier to lead her away. As he left Valerie glared after him, hate in her eyes.

"OK, seriously, what happened to you guys?" Karen demanded.

Valerie grabbed the spoon from the tub and helped herself to a heaping scoop of ice cream. "Let's just say we didn't get the warmest of welcomes." She turned to Krasinski. "You work here, right? Well top tip, hot shot," she said, her voice muffled with her mouth full. "When your boys interrogate someone like me they should stick to *black* or *African American* if they feel the need to talk about my race. When they decide to go off script they shouldn't be surprised if they get a slap in the face."

Krasinski cringed uncomfortably, his cheeks glowing with embarrassment. "I'm terribly sorry, ma'am" he said, taking a seat on the other side of the table. "We have a zero tolerance policy for that kind of behavior. If you'd like to file a complaint with the base I'd be more than happy to…" His voice trailed off as he realized how ridiculous he sounded. "Well, I don't suppose much would come of it, given the current circumstances."

"Probably not, no," Valerie scowled, digging the spoon into the ice cream. "So let's just put it down to a regrettable slip of the tongue and move on."

"Guys, this is Ted Krasinski," Karen said, eager to move the conversation to safer ground. "He's a… a lawyer, I think? He's going to tell us what's been going on while we were on the road. Ted, you wanna just jump right in?"

"Thank you," Krasinski nodded. "And thank *you*." He smiled up at a member of the mess staff as she placed a tray on the table. He gratefully grabbed a fresh cup of coffee, shook out two sachets of sugar into the mug, and his hand hovered over a third before he thought better of it.

"Actually, I'm not a lawyer," he eventually began, cradling the mug in his hands as he blew across the surface, apparently enjoying the attention of his captive audience. "I'm an accountant. A forensic accountant, to be exact, working for the DoD. It's my job to make sure that your tax dollars go exactly where they're supposed to go."

He took a sip, cringed, and reached for the third sugar. "I check for… y'know, irregularities in the books. Unexplained hammers that cost twenty five grand, accrued vacation pay for staff who retired ten years ago, that sort of thing. You'd be amazed to learn how often people try to skim a little off the top, even when they know the military courts will come down on them much harder than any civilian court. In fact, one time I found a lieutenant who…"

He waved a hand, sensing he was losing his audience. "Well, maybe that's a story for another time. Anyway… a couple of months ago I was called out to Travis AFB to investigate a number of outgoing payments the local staff couldn't explain. Mostly just small stuff, random invoices issued in the thousands of dollars, small enough to go unnoticed unless you were auditing the accounts. It looked like someone at the base was trying to set themselves up with a nice unofficial retirement fund."

He set down his mug. "*So what,* you might ask. There must be a ton of theft and fraud going on in the military, and you'd be right to think that. People skim millions of dollars from the military every year.

Tens of millions, in fact, but the kind of people who try to rip off the government usually understand the massive risks involved, and they tend not to half ass it. They don't just write themselves a check from a military account and hope nobody will notice. Most of them are smart enough to bury what they're doing so deep that nobody ever find out."

Krasinski tapped the sheaf of papers that sat in front of him. "*These* transfers, though, didn't fit the usual pattern at all. They were just *brazen* theft. Someone was skimming money from base operational accounts, the same accounts they use to pay the utility bills and keep the bathrooms stocked with toilet paper, and as far as I could tell they barely made even a token effort to hide it. The transfers were right there, plain as day in the account statements, as obvious as stealing a six pack of beer from a grocery store, strolling past the security guard and then coming back five minutes later to grab a bag of nuts. As far as theft goes this was just *next level* stupid."

He took a sip of his coffee, shaking his head. "OK, so far so dumb. If you were just a regular base accountant you'd probably figure some dumbass was trying to skim cash without really knowing what he was doing. You'd cancel the payments, report it to your superior and forget about it. But here's the thing that struck me as odd." He leaned forward and lowered his voice. "This wasn't going on at just one base. As soon as I reported the Travis accounts I started to hear reports about similar things happening at bases right across the country, in every branch. Air Force bases here in California. A Navy shipyard out in Maine. Even a National Guard recruiting station in Wisconsin. There were more than two dozen bases involved, each of them sending out regular small payments, and all of them were going to the same recipient."

Ramos leaned in, lowering his voice to match Krasinski's. "Where was the money going?"

"That's the weird thing," Krasinski replied. "The paper trail told us the payments were being made to a consulting firm in Maryland by the name of Reagan Wilkes Global, but when I tracked it down I found it was just three college grads working out of a strip mall a few miles outside Annapolis. They had no *clue* about any payments coming from the military. They didn't even have any *connections* to the military, and they had no idea they had millions of dollars sitting in the bank in their name. They barely had enough money to buy breakfast at the Taco Bell next door."

"What, you just took them at their word?" Karen interjected, skeptically raising her eyebrows.

"Their word?" Krasinski laughed. "Lord, no. I'm an accountant. When it comes to money I wouldn't take my own mother at her word. No, I came down on those kids like a ton of bricks. I went through their books with a fine toothed comb, and by the time I was done I was absolutely *certain* they were on the level. They genuinely had no idea the account existed. As far as I could make out someone had set it up in their name, all legit, all apparently legal, but with no real connection to the company or its owners. They probably just picked the name out of the Yellow Pages and maybe stole some ID and mail to set up the account, just so there was a legitimate business connected to the invoices."

"So," he continued, "it looked like I was dealing with someone who was either mind meltingly dumb or, and this is where it gets interesting, someone who wasn't all that worried about getting caught. That's what I figured at first. This theft was so obvious, so easy to detect, that I figured maybe it was someone who knew he only had a few months to live. You know, maybe some accounts clerk with access to base funds who wanted to treat himself to a fancy vacation before the cancer finished him off. But that's not the most interesting part."

Ramos nodded, urging him to get on with it. "So what was the most interesting part?"

Krasinski once again set down his mug, and a sly smile spread across his face. "Surprise twist. Up until now I'd only been looking at one side of the books. I was focused on the debits, because that's where the problem was. It never occurred to me to look at the credit column, but as soon as I took a look I realized this thing went a lot deeper than I'd suspected. See, the funds were always returned in full exactly three days after they were deposited. Every penny of every last payment, like clockwork." He brought his fists to his temples and then spread them out, mimicking the sound of an explosion. "Mind blown, right? Right?"

"Ted," Karen said in a slow, patient tone, "remember you're not speaking at a convention of forensic accountants here, OK? We have no idea what this means."

"Don't you see?" Krasinski narrowed his eyes and spoke in a hushed, excited whisper. "Nobody was actually stealing the money. They never actually *stole* a single cent. Someone was orchestrating a massive transfer of funds into this secret account, but they weren't spending any of it. They weren't even *keeping* it. I found payments going back eight months, thousands of them, and every last cent was returned to the base from whence it came. After three days the money landed right back in the operational accounts as if it had never left. Whoever was in charge of this thing set it up to make it look like the payments were automatically bounced, as if the transfers had failed."

"OK," Karen nodded, too exhausted to try to make sense of what Ted was saying. "But why is any of this important?"

"I'm getting to it," Krasinski assured her. "Trust me, this will all make sense when you hear about the ship."

Valerie narrowed her eyes. "Wait a second," she slowly muttered, and everyone jumped in their seats as she slapped her hand on the table and cried out. "The ship! I *knew* I'd heard your voice somewhere. You're the guy on the radio!"

"I'm sorry?" Krasinski shook his head, confused. "What radio?"

"Last night! That was you on the VHF band, right? You were calling from Travis, asking to speak to… what's his name? Colonel MacAuliffe! You said you had evidence that the nukes were dropped by Americans!"

"*Quiet!*" Krasinski leaned in and whispered harshly as the color drained from his face. "That's classified information. *Jesus.* You were eavesdropping on me?"

"Damn right I was eavesdropping. There's no law against it."

"Of course there's a law against it!" Krasinski hissed, but his indignant tone evaporated in the face of Valerie's confidence. "Seriously? Are… are you sure? Seems like there should be."

"Nope. As long as you don't interfere you can listen in on any radio signal you can pick up. If you don't want people listening you shouldn't broadcast in the clear. You should know better. Military comms are supposed to be encrypted."

"I had no choice!" insisted Krasinski, his tone suddenly defensive. "The blasts knocked out our satellite comms, so we're down to VHF line-of-sight until we can get the system back on its feet."

"Hey, it's not my ass that'll get court-martialed for broadcasting classified material on a frequency truckers can pick up." She glared at Krasinski for a moment, watching him fall to pieces before her eyes, and then she shot him a wink as a mischievous grin spread across her face. "Oh, unbunch your panties, Ted. I'm just screwing with you. If even half of what you said was true, we have bigger things to worry about right now."

"Half of *what?*" Karen demanded, trying to keep up. "What's this about a ship?"

Krasinski took a moment to gather himself, but it was clear the wind had been taken out of his sails. Until now he'd been enjoying telling the story, but now he looked like he had a rod down the back of his shirt, speaking as if he were on the witness stand.

"Yes, the ship," he continued, coughing awkwardly. "Or *ships*, plural, to be precise. For weeks I struggled to understand what might be the purpose of the Reagan Wilkes account. I couldn't fathom why anyone would go to all this trouble just to move some money around, especially when I learned that this particular account accrued no interest. There didn't seem to be any obvious rhyme or reason to the thing, and it was only when I secured a warrant for the account records that it started to make sense."

He glanced around the mess, making sure there was nobody within earshot. "See, the people behind this weren't interested in the money at all. At any one time there was always at least two million dollars resting in the account, but since the day the account was opened nobody had made a single withdrawal. What I finally figured out was that they only wanted the balance itself. They were using it as collateral to secure lines of credit. They wanted to make it appear as if they had enough funds to cover purchases of a few hundred grand, and they were doing it without *technically* stealing a single cent from the government."

"And they were buying ships?" Karen asked.

"Yes. Freighters, in fact. Outdated, rusty cargo ships earmarked for scrap. From the evidence I pieced together I learned that they bought eight small freighters in the last six months, all of them from operators in countries such as Azerbaijan and Côte d'Ivoire, where financial regulations are treated more like polite suggestions, and all of them on credit using the misappropriated funds as collateral."

"But why? Why would someone go to so much trouble just to buy some rusty old ships?"

Krasinski threw up his hands. "That's where I hit a dead end. I'm an accountant, not a cop. My job was only to follow the money and see where it led, but for me that was the end of it. I'm not paid to worry about motives. As soon as I'd canceled the outgoing payments and confirmed that every penny had been accounted for I cracked open a beer and slapped myself on the back. I'd solved my part of the mystery. It was a job well done."

He fell silent for a moment, a haunted look suddenly flitting across his face. "Or at least it *was,* until I turned on the TV yesterday and watched General Reynolds give his briefing from the Pentagon. As soon as I heard the name of the ship I felt the hairs on the back of my neck stand to attention."

"You mean the ship that blew up out in the Pacific? That was– "

"The *MC Nakharov,*" Krasinski nodded solemnly. "It was an old cargo ship that spent twenty years crossing the Black Sea between Trabzon and Sevastopol. It was decommissioned after its keel was damaged last year, and it was due to be tugged to the Aliaga breaking yard in Turkey when a mystery buyer snapped it up with a loan note for a couple hundred thousand dollars. It fell off the radar for a few months, and then yesterday it popped up out of the clear blue sky off the west coast, sailing under a Panamanian flag and registered to a shell company in

Karachi, which was in turn owned by another shell based out of Moscow."

"The Russians?" Ramos scratched his stubble. "You mean they had a hand in this?"

Krasinski shook his head. "No, not at all. Or at least I don't think they did. Someone just wanted to make it *look* as if they were involved, and it was the same story with the other half dozen ships that arrived off the coast along with the *Nakharov*. They were registered to companies everywhere from Riyadh to Damascus to Dalian, China, a stone's throw from the North Korean border, but the trails all led back to Moscow."

He grabbed his mug and held it close to his chest, as if comforting himself with the warmth. "Someone went to a hell of a lot of trouble to send us chasing our tails. They threw out what a cop would call an orgy of evidence, a dozen different threads that lead everywhere but the real culprit. The way I see it someone desperately wants us to believe that this attack came from Moscow, or Pyongyang, or the Saudis. They want us confused and paranoid. If I hadn't stumbled on the Reagan Wilkes account I would have fallen for it." He poked a finger at the papers. "But thanks to this evidence I can prove that the money trail leads right back here. Right to our doorstep. I can prove that those ships were bought by someone connected to our own military."

"So it was really us? We really did this to ourselves?"

Krasinski nodded. "It looks that way, yeah, though I've no idea why."

"You said there were eight ships, but only seven of them showed up on the coast. What happened to the other one?"

"Well," Krasinski replied, "one of them was lost in a storm somewhere off the coast of Mauritania late last year. I guess if you're buying junk you run the risk of losing them."

Ramos listlessly poked at the ice cream with a spoon, deep in thought. "What about the nukes?" he asked. "Anyone can buy a bunch of old boats, but I'm guessing you need more than a shady bank account to get your hands on nuclear weapons."

"Yeah," Krasinski agreed. "That's where I have to admit defeat. The Reagan Wilkes account is just part of the puzzle, I'm sure. I don't know anything about nuclear weapons, or how anyone could get hold of them. All I know is that I need to get this evidence to someone higher up the chain of command before we go and do something stupid."

"Stupid like what?" Ramos asked.

Krasinski frowned. "Stupid like launching our nuclear arsenal at Moscow or Riyadh in retaliation for an attack that had nothing to do with them. I don't know what's going on in Washington right now, but you can bet they're looking for someone to bomb. The entire country will be baying for blood. The government needs a villain, and with all the evidence I'm sure they won't have any trouble finding one. We could be looking at the outbreak of World War Three."

"Jesus," Karen whispered, staring at the sheaf of papers in front of Krasinski. It was hard to believe that the future of humanity could rest on a bunch of bank statements. "Wait. If you need to get this up the chain of command how come you're just sitting around here with us? Haven't you shown this to the base commander?"

"Here at Beale?" Krasinski nodded. "I tried, but most of the base personnel have been sent to Truckee to manage the safe zone. Right now the most senior officer at Beale is a twenty five year old first lieutenant, and he's so out of his depth he hasn't left his office since this morning. I tried to reach Colonel

MacAuliffe on the radio last night, but they wouldn't put me through. By the time I arrived he'd already left for Truckee."

"They wouldn't put you through to him for *this*?" Karen scoffed. "You should have insisted!"

"I should have insisted?" Krasinski gave her a withering look. "I'm not sure what you know about the military chain of command, but it goes a little something like this." He raised his hand as high as he could reach. "Right up here you've got your generals, colonels and majors, OK?" He lowered his hand an inch. "And here you've got your captains, lieutenants and your enlisted men. Now *all* the way down here," he dropped his hand slowly beneath the table, "you've got your janitors and mess hall staff, and just beneath *them* you'll find the accountants. I'm a civilian attached to the DoD. I don't even have a rank. Someone like me doesn't just *insist* on speaking to a colonel."

"OK, I take your point," Karen grudgingly conceded. "So where do you go from here?"

"Well, all I can do now is try to find an officer with half a brain." He tapped the pages in front of him. "I'm waiting for a spot on a transport out to Truckee. I need someone who can understand what all of this means, and has the ability to relay the information higher up the chain. We need to get this stuff to Washington, but until we can reestablish the satellite link all we have is line of sight comms and limited cell phone reception. It's not like we can– "

His voice trailed off when he noticed a low hum from his pocket. "Sorry, I have to take this," he said, pulling out his cell phone. "I'll just be– "

"Hang on," Karen interrupted. "You have cell phone reception?"

'Well, yeah. Beale has its own cell tower. Only local calls. It's a little hit and miss because most of the west coast network is down, but if you manage to connect to a working base station you might get lucky."

Karen turned to Ramos and grabbed him by the arm. "Doc, do you still have my phone?"

Ramos frowned, digging around in his pockets. "Ummm... yeah, I think you put it in with the meds when you got in the car, right?" He pulled out the plastic bag and sifted through the contents. "Yeah, here it is."

Karen snatched the phone from his hand, and her eyes lit up as she activated the screen and saw three bars showing in the signal indicator, though her excitement was tempered a little by the sight of the battery indicator. 6% remaining.

"Ted," she said, waving her hand in front of his face. "Sorry, Ted, please, just a second."

Krasinski cupped his hand over the microphone and shot her an impatient glare. "I'm on the phone."

"I'm sorry, I just need to know if we'll be allowed to leave here. We need to get to the safe zone in Truckee."

Krasinski nodded. "Of course. You're civilians, you can't stay here. As soon as your daughter gets back they'll drive you out to highway 20 and cut you loose. In fact, if you try to come back they'll shoot you." He pointed at his phone. "Is it OK if I get back to my call now?"

"Sure. Sorry." Karen narrowed her eyes, wondering if he was joking about the shooting thing, but she was too excited to worry about it. She tapped the screen, brought up Jack's number and pressed the phone against her ear as the call tried to connect.

Sorry, we are unable to connect your call at this time. Please try again.

"Damn," she hissed tapping the screen to redial. "It's not going through."

Sorry, we are unable to–

She sighed, dropping the phone to the table. "Stupid piece of crap. Jack must be out of range."

"That must be it." Ramos gave her a sympathetic smile. "Or maybe his battery ran out."

Karen shot him a sidelong glance, and under her steely gaze Ramos grabbed the spoon and poked at the ice cream. He didn't want to look her in the eye, and it wasn't hard to see why. She knew what he was thinking.

If he's even still alive.

"Just say it, Doc."

Ramos scooped a spoonful and let it fall back into the tub. "Say what?"

"I know what you're thinking," Karen snapped, snatching the spoon from his hand. "If you think he's dead, just say it."

"Dead?" Ramos sighed, and before he answered he took a moment to compose his thoughts. Finally he laid his hand on her shoulder and looked her straight in the eye. "Karen," he said, "I've known Jack since he was a first year resident, and hand to God I've never met a more stubborn, tenacious, bloody minded pain in the ass in all my years in medicine. I'm not going to lie to you. It's hell out there, and he has a lot of miles to cover if he's going to make it back to us, but

I know this for sure. If there's one guy who could make it halfway across the country while nukes are blowing up around him it's Jack Archer. He cares too much to even *think* about giving up. That man would walk through fire if Emily was on the other side."

Karen felt tears prick at her eyes, and when Ramos spoke again she struggled to hold them back.

"He'd walk through fire for you, too." Ramos began to blush. It was clear he was out of his comfort zone, but he forced himself to go on. He could see that she needed to hear this. "He never stopped loving you, Karen. Not for a minute. Not even when things got really bad. When I spoke to him yesterday I could hear the love in his voice. I didn't have to ask him to come home."

Karen clutched the phone tighter, fighting to keep her lip from wobbling. She knew she'd burst into tears if she let her guard down.

"So no, I don't think he's dead," Ramos continued. "I think he's running just as fast as he can to get back to the two of you, and when he hears from you it'll only make him run harder. Send him a message. If he still has his phone he'll find a way to read it."

"What should I say?" Karen asked, her voice

trembling as she fought to hold back her emotions.

"Tell him…" Ramos scratched at the thick gray stubble sprouting on his cheeks. "Tell him we'll meet him at the safe zone. Send him to Truckee. Tell him his girls are waiting for him there." He squeezed her shoulder and gave her a reassuring smile. "Tell him you love him."

Karen nodded, wiping a tear from her cheek as she looked down at the phone, and with a shuddering breath she began to type.

•▼•

CHAPTER FOUR
48 MILES TO TRUCKEE

THE MILES SEEMED to pass beneath the wheels in a blur.

For the past hour Jack had been fighting to keep his attention fixed on the road ahead. He struggled to keep his eyes from wandering back to the cell phone on the dash, but each time the winding ribbon of asphalt straightened he succumbed to the temptation. He just couldn't help but steal another glance at the words that had sent his heart thumping a samba rhythm the moment he'd seen them.

On any other day he'd drive at a cautious crawl on a treacherous road like this, a series of tight switchbacks high in the Sierra Nevadas. He'd usually drive with one foot hovering over the brake, muttering under his breath at suicidal drivers as they roared by on blind hairpin bends. A whispered prayer would never be far from his lips as he hugged the shoulder, keeping as far as possible from the dizzying drop on the far side of the road.

But not today. Today he urged the stolen police cruiser onward ever faster, his foot glued to the gas pedal. Even when he reached the tight hairpin turns he kept going at breakneck speed, touching the brake only as an occasional afterthought, veering out so close to the steel barrier that he could reach out and touch it. Still he wanted to go faster, and the throaty V8 growled its eager encouragement.

A brief straight appeared at the end of a broad, sweeping curve, and without a second thought Jack grabbed his phone from the dash and tapped back to the message, staring at the screen as if he still didn't quite believe it was real.

Me+Em+Doc heading to safe zone in Truckee. We're safe. Can you meet us there? Please tell us where you are.

We both love you so, so much xxx

Please come home to us.

K

As soon as he'd seen the message on the way out of Plumas Creek he'd felt every last muscle in his body relax. He hadn't realized just how tightly wound the fear had left him, how on edge he'd been, not knowing whether Karen and Emily were alive or dead. When he saw those words he'd felt a wave of excitement rush through his body, and without thinking he'd stepped on the gas and sent the cruiser surging forward.

And then something else had happened, something he'd never expected at his age. As he played the words over in his head he discovered that in the blink of an eye he regressed to the state of an anxious lovestruck teen. He'd pulled the cruiser to the side of the road, clicked away and opened the first message Karen had sent, comparing the two with forensic obsession while Cathy protested from the back seat.

Love you

We both love you so, so much xxx

He'd pored over that first message a thousand times over the last twenty four hours, wondering if

Karen had written those words with genuine love or just out of habit, a muscle memory hangover after years of marriage. For hours he'd tortured himself with the possibilities of those words, poking at them like a tongue against a loose tooth.

And now it looked as if he finally had an answer. The second message seemed unambiguous. Karen hadn't typed those words absently. They weren't just a meaningless pleasantry.

She still loves you.

The thought of it had plastered a delirious grin on his face. It had been more than a year since the night he'd packed his bags and left the family home. A year since that last argument, the straw that broke the camel's back, when Karen brought Emily home from school and found Jack slumped on the sofa in the basement, an empty bottle of scotch and loose Percocet scattered across the floor beside him. He'd only been half conscious as she yelled at him, staring at her through glazed eyes, but he'd sobered up when he saw the look on her face. When he saw her flip that mental switch as she made the decision that ended their marriage.

I can't afford to love you any more. It's killing me.

Every moment since then he'd felt as if there were

a wall standing between him and his family, ten feet thick and a hundred tall, impossible to breach. He thought he was cursed to spend the rest of his life standing out in the cold while his little girl was raised in the warm glow of her mother's love, a love he'd so selfishly rejected as he indulged himself in pity and drank to silence the guilt and shame.

But now... now for the first time he thought he could see a chink of light break through that wall.

He'd feverishly tapped out a response, pouring out his heart in a few dozen characters. He'd barely been able to control his excitement, ignoring Cathy as she yelled at him to get moving, but when he hit send it had only taken a few seconds for the message to bounce back.

Delivery failed.

He'd tried again and again, first tapping the screen and then angrily stabbing at it, but each time the phone kicked back the same maddening error message as the signal indicator wavered between a single bar and zero. Even when he wheeled the cruiser around and drove back to the exact spot the message had come through the phone refused to cooperate. It was as if they'd passed through a magical sweet spot, a shifting square inch of air where the signal was just strong enough to carry a message, but when Jack tried to find it again it eluded him, like an itch that came from deep beneath the skin where searching fingernails couldn't reach it.

An hour had passed since then, and Jack still couldn't help but stare at the screen every couple of minutes, praying for a signal to appear.

"It's beautiful, isn't it?"

The question hung in the air for a long moment before Jack realized it had been directed at him.

"Huh? Sorry, what was that?" He grabbed hold of the rear view mirror and angled it towards the back seat. Cathy lay curled up with Boomer against the door, grabbing some much needed sleep after her night outdoors. Beside her Garside leaned forward between the front seats, gazing out the windshield at the pine forest that whipped by on either side of the road.

"I said it's quite beautiful, isn't it? The view, I mean."

He took a deep breath and let out a long, peaceful sigh, and Jack flinched away from the smell of whiskey on his breath. Cathy had added a more than generous splash to the cup of gas station coffee they'd poured down his throat back when they'd stopped back in Greenville, and it seemed to have done the trick. Gone was the shocked, trembling shell of a man who replayed over and over the moment he'd killed the sheriff. Now Garside seemed like a new man, serene and at peace, and since he'd grabbed the bottle and continued to drink in the car he'd become ever more at peace as the journey continued. Perhaps a little too much.

"Yeah, I guess it's pretty damned beautiful," Jack agreed, though he'd barely noticed the scenery as he split his attention between the phone and the road.

"You know, I had no idea your country could look so bloody spectacular," Garside smiled, shaking his head in wonder at the endless pine forest that climbed from the shadows of the deep gorges to the peaks that towered above them. "Back home... back home we think we know America. Most of us only know about it through movies and TV shows, and I think a lot of us come away with the impression that your entire country is... I don't know, just a bunch of scary rednecks in small towns and sarcastic liberals in the cities. Fast food and fat people as far as the eye can see. I know that's what *I* thought before I came here."

"Well thanks, Doug," Jack grimaced, shying away

from the pungent odor of whiskey. "You really know how to flatter a patriot."

"No, no, that's not what I mean," Garside slurred. "I mean we just get a strange, skewed snapshot of your country that doesn't look anything like reality. We get our heads filled with that nonsense and we think it's real."

He sighed again, resting his chin on the head rest in front of him, a peaceful, slightly soused smile plastered across his face. "But then we see a place like this. These mountains. That sky. Good Lord, I see a view like this and suddenly I understand why you people wave your flags so much. Did you ever see anything quite so beautiful?"

Jack looked out on the scenery, really *seeing* it for the first time. The bright sunlight shining from a crisp, clear blue sky gave the sprawling pine forest a rich emerald sheen. As the road curved around a rocky outcrop a swift, narrow river came into view far below, white water churning at the foot of a gorge, working its way between immovable boulders as it searched for lower ground. Far above their heads a brace of eagles swooped around each other in slow, stately arcs, searching for prey in the forest clearings below. It looked like the kind of place where taking a single deep breath of the crisp, clean air would cure any illness. It really *was* picture postcard beautiful.

"Twice," he muttered, looking back on a distant memory. "I've only seen beauty like this twice before."

Jack glanced in the rear view, and he smiled at Garside's questioning expression.

"My kids," he explained. "The day they were born. Nothing compares to the first time you see them. It's just… I can't describe the feeling. Looking down at this perfect little thing and thinking Jesus… I *made* this. Takes your breath away, and you don't ever really get it back."

"Ah, yes," smiled Garside, "I know that feeling well." He tipped the whiskey back, wincing as it burned his throat. "Until that moment comes you can't really understand what your heart is for."

Jack was surprised. "You have kids?" For some reason he hadn't imagined Doug as a parent. Hadn't even considered the possibility that there might be a whole family of Garsides back home.

"Oh, I'll say. We have three, two girls and a boy. Well, I suppose I should say two women and a man now. Our youngest flew the coop last year, down to London to either follow her dreams or work at Pret a

Manger, whichever takes the least effort."

He paused for a moment, gazing at the whiskey with a sigh before he continued, his tone suddenly maudlin. "To be honest I think Brenda and I have been at something of a loose end since they left. It's hard to adjust to an empty nest after so many years, you know? Hard to walk through the house and find it silent after a couple of decades of laughter and tears. I suppose that's why we made this trip, now I think about it. Just… just trying to fill the time." He moved to take another swig from the bottle, and suddenly froze. "Good Lord, where are my manners?" He thrust the open bottle over the seat, tapping it against Jack's shoulder. "Care for a nip?"

"I'm good, thanks," Jack replied, turning his head and holding his breath to avoid the smell. "Not while I'm driving. I want to keep a clear head."

He'd just blurted out the first refusal that came to mind, but as soon as he spoke the words he realized they were true. He *was* good. In fact, he was better than he'd been in as long as he could remember. He couldn't remember the last time he'd turned down a drink.

He didn't want to kid himself. Sure, he'd love nothing more than to pull over and drain the bottle, to escape into that wonderful and terrible oblivion for a few hours. He knew there wasn't a simple switch he could flip to turn off the cravings. He knew he'd have a lifetime of temptation ahead of him, and he had no idea if he'd always be able to find the strength to resist, but right now he felt a pull in the other direction, and it was a thousand times stronger than the pull of the bottle.

It was coming from his phone. He reached out and tapped it, awaking the screen to flash its message of hope. The tether pulling him back to his past, and towards one possible future.

We both love you so, so much xxx

"What about you?"

"Hmmm?" Jack half turned to Garside, still resting his chin on the passenger seat.

"Your kids. I'm guessing you're not old enough to have turfed them out of the house yet?"

"Oh. No, they're still little. Emily's seven. Well, she'd want me to tell you she's seven and three quarters." He grinned. "Her mom started teaching her fractions a little while ago, and now she insists. Robbie…" He paused for a moment. He didn't want to have this conversation again. "Robbie's six. The most beautiful little angel you could ever imagine. Always smiling."

"And you and their mother, you're not... you're not together?" Garside screwed the cap back on the bottle and slipped it into the pocket in the back of the driver's seat. "Sorry, I don't mean to pry. I just got the impression that maybe you were..."

"Yeah, we're divorced. Long story. I wasn't the greatest husband those last couple of years. Wasn't a very good father, either. I took a few wrong turns, and then a few more, and before I knew it... well, I guess I found myself somewhere I didn't want to be."

Garside patted him on the shoulder. "I'm sorry to hear that, Jack."

"Thanks, Doug." Jack squinted out at the road. Up ahead was a junction, and as they drew closer he saw two signposts: Marysville 60 miles to the right, Truckee 48 to the left. He swung the wheel and sent the cruiser left.

"I don't want to jinx it," he said, pressing his foot hard on the gas, "but after all this time I think I've finally remembered the way home."

Forty eight miles to Karen and Emily. With a full tank of gas and a following wind, even on these slow, winding roads they were no more than an hour from the safe zone. An hour from wrapping his arms around his little girl and never letting go. He didn't want to get ahead of himself, but maybe an hour away from a future he thought was gone forever. Tonight he wouldn't be sleeping alone in a hotel room far from home. He wouldn't wake up hungover with the other half of the bed ice cold. He'd be with his family for the first time in… *God, more than a year?* The longing felt like a fist squeezing his heart.

For the first time in a long time Jack felt something he thought had abandoned him long ago. *Hope*. In the middle of all this horror, in amongst all the death and destruction, he felt like a bright beacon of optimism. Even now he could see the future roll out ahead of him. When they reached the safe zone Garside could contact the zones east of Los Angeles and track down his wife. Maybe – God willing she survived the attack – they could arrange for her to be sent further inland. Maybe they could all travel east together, back to a part of the country where life was still going on. Where they could find shelter and start to rebuild. Maybe they could–

"Jack, do you hear that?"

"Huh?" Garside's voice pulled Jack from his

reverie. "What did you say?"

"Listen." Doug held up a hand. "Is it just me, or do you hear a horn?"

Jack tilted his head. For a moment he could only hear the shrill whistle of wind through the narrowly opened window beside him, but then he caught it at the very edge of his hearing. A long, insistent honk sounded in the distance, and it only grew louder as he rolled the window fully down.

"Is that ahead of us or behind?" he asked, shifting the rear view to get a better angle out the back window. "Do you see anything?"

"No, I..." Garside twisted in his seat, peering out the rear windshield as the cruiser turned around a switchback. "*Wait!* Yes, I caught a glimpse of something behind us just before we went round that bend. A pickup truck or a van, I think. Something big, anyway. Looked like it was taking up half the road."

"What color was it, Doug?"

"I... oh, I'm not sure. I only saw it for a second and it was too far away to make out, but I think... brown or gray, maybe?"

"Shit," Jack hissed, feeling goosebumps prickle across his skin as he stepped harder on the gas, urging the cruiser forward as fast as he dared. Back at Plumas Creek the sheriff's friend had been driving an old beige pickup. But *surely* it couldn't be him? The town was almost two hours drive behind them, and when they'd left the guy had still been out cold on the asphalt. Could he really be so bloody minded that he'd chase them a hundred miles across the Sierra Nevadas just to get revenge?

"Cathy." He turned in his seat and shook her leg. "*Cathy!* Wake up. We've got company."

Cathy frowned, half asleep and mumbling. "What?"

"Wake up! We might have trouble on the way."

Finally she opened her eyes, bloodshot and glazed. "Jesus, Jack, can't a girl sleep for five minutes?" She stretched in her seat, gently pushing Boomer from her lap as her hand slipped down to the holster at her hip. "What is it?"

"Someone's coming up behind us. Doug says a pickup, maybe brown or gray."

"Oh, God," she moaned, pulling out her pistol. "You don't think it's Ray, do you?"

Jack shrugged. "I don't know, but it sounds like we're about to find out. He's gaining on us." The driver was still honking his horn, only now it sounded much closer, maybe just a couple of turns behind them on the tightly winding road.

"Damn it." Cathy turned and looked out the rear window. "If we'd been thinking straight we would have tossed his keys into the forest before we left."

Jack grimaced, his eyes locked on the road ahead. "If we'd been thinking straight we would have shot him in the head." He scanned the road, searching for a good ambush spot. "We have to stop him before he catches us. Do you think you could shoot out the tires if I stop the car?"

Cathy lifted her pistol. "With this? No, I'm pretty sure that only works in the movies. I'd need a clean shot through the side wall. If I got lucky I might hit one tire, but there'd be no guarantee it'd deflate right away, and even if it did there's no guarantee it would be enough to stop him."

"How about the engine? Maybe a shot through the radiator? You think that could be enough to kill it?"

Cathy shook her head. "I wouldn't want to bet my life on it. With a 9MM it'd take a lucky shot or a couple of magazines to do enough damage to knock out the engine. And just in case you were thinking to ask, gas tanks don't explode when you shoot them."

"Damn it." Jack slapped his palm against the wheel

with frustration. The honking was even louder now, almost constant, and he knew they only had a minute or two before the vehicle caught up with them. He spun the wheel and sent the car careening around a tight hairpin at a rocky outcrop, and as the road straightened out again Cathy grabbed his shoulder.

"*Pull in here!*" she yelled, pointing to a spot just after the turn where the road widened a little. Jack stamped on the brake without thinking, steering the cruiser into the shadow of the rock wall that loomed over the road, and it wasn't until the car had screeched to a halt that he wondered why he'd followed her order.

"Why are we stopping? I thought you couldn't stop the truck with that thing."

"I'm not going to stop the truck, Jack," she said, pushing open her door and climbing out. "He has to slow down to take the turn, and he won't see us until he's almost on top of us." She dropped into a crouch at the front of the cruiser, resting her elbows on the hood, pointing the pistol at the road behind them. "When he comes around the corner I'm gonna shoot him through the windshield."

Jack looked back at the bend, expecting the pickup to rocket into sight at any moment. "Well, wait a minute. Are you sure you can make that shot?"

Cathy nodded, closing one eye and staring down the barrel. "Don't worry, Jack, a baby could make this shot. He'll be a big, slow moving target."

Jack decided not to press the point, but that wasn't what he meant. He wasn't asking her if she could *hit* the target. He was asking if she was ready to take a life. He'd never done it before, and God willing he'd never have to, but he was pretty sure there was a yawning gulf between putting a bullet through a paper target and putting one through a man's chest. If Cathy hesitated when the moment came…

He could hear the engine now, a ghostly echo bouncing off the rocky walls of the gorge, and he reached to the glove compartment and pulled out the sheriff's revolver, resting it in his lap just in case it came down to a firefight. He was fairly sure he wouldn't have the guts to pull the trigger if it came down to it, but he felt better just knowing that the gun was there.

The pickup was just around the corner now. Whatever happened from here on in, it was too late now to change course. Jack whispered a prayer and kept his foot hovering over the gas as he saw Cathy's hands tremble. He knew they wouldn't get far, but he was ready to drive if she lost her nerve.

With a squeal of brakes followed by the high pitched whine of a low gear the vehicle came racing into view around the bend, and as soon as Jack caught sight of it he felt a rush of relief, followed immediately by a wave of dread.

It wasn't Ray's pickup.

It wasn't a pickup at all.

It was a military Humvee, a tan camouflage painted monster that took up most of the narrow road, and as soon as it came into view around the hairpin bend everything seemed to shift into slow motion. Jack could see the surprise in the face of the driver. It was clear he hadn't expected to find the cruiser hiding around the corner. He slammed on the brakes. With a deafening squeal the enormous tires locked up, and the vehicle went into a sideways, shimmying skid before crashing to a halt against the steel crash barrier at the edge of the road.

Before the vehicle came to a stop, though, Cathy squeezed the trigger. She was already committed to it. Her trigger finger got the message to pull before her brain had the chance to call a cease fire. Jack flinched at the report, and he felt his heart jump into his throat as a white blemish appeared in the toughened glass of the Humvee's windshield, inches from the driver's face.

He turned back to Cathy in time to see the shock spread across her face. She looked down at the gun as if she had no idea what it was doing in her hands, and as the passenger side door of the Humvee swung open she tossed it to the ground and raised both arms in the air.

"*Don't shoot!*" she yelled, her eyes bulging with terror. "*I didn't mean it!*"

Jack instinctively ducked in his seat when he saw a pair of boots hit the ground beside the truck. A uniformed man stepped out into the road, his pistol drawn as he shielded himself behind his open door. For a long moment he watched Cathy through the narrow gap between the door frame, and then he began to step towards the cruiser, his gun raised.

"*You!*" He yelled, pointing the gun squarely at Cathy's chest. "*Down on the ground!*"

•▼•

CHAPTER FIVE
THE WHIRLY THING ON TOP

BEALE AIR FORCE Base looked nothing like Karen had pictured.

She'd expected it to be busier. She'd imagined rows of fighter jets lined up ready for takeoff, and hangars full of men in flight suits flashing semaphore at each other. Now that she thought about it she realized she'd pictured a scene from Top Gun, but the reality… well, it wasn't quite so spectacular.

As she walked out the door tightly clutching Emily's hand she looked back at the hunched, single story administrative building where they'd been holding her, and from this angle it looked almost exactly like a rundown suburban high school. Beside it sat a plot of hundreds of small homes laid out in a grid, each identical in every way, from the white picket fences to the sun-bleached red paint on the wooden walls. Beyond that there was nothing at all. Barren scrub seemed to stretch all the way to the distant horizon.

"I thought it'd be more… I don't know, more impressive," she remarked. "Where are all the planes?"

The officer striding ahead of her replied without turning. "Beale is a 23,000 acre site, ma'am. It's home to the 9th Reconnaissance Wing and a hell of a lot of classified UAVs, and we don't show our toys to visitors. Please, this way."

He led them around the corner of the admin building and pointed towards a large prefab garage built from corrugated sheets. As soon as Karen saw it the memories came flooding back, and her heart began to flutter in her chest.

"Right back where we started," she sighed, noticing the troop truck parked in the center of the garage. It was the same truck that had brought them to the base. The same truck she'd been dragged from, kicking and screaming. Now she saw it she remembered being carried, half insensible, across the open ground to the admin building, and the memories hit her without mercy.

She remembered the tone of her voice changing as they dragged her out of the truck. Her scream began muffled by the canvas and ended with an eerie echo, bouncing off the corrugated walls. She remembered the pain as she landed on the hard concrete floor. The thick stink of diesel clawing its way down her throat. The pinch of hands grabbing her beneath her arms, and the changing sound as her heels dragged from the concrete out onto the dust outside.

And then... then the pain. The agony as the butt of the rifle knocked her senseless. The choking sensation as she fell face first into the dust, breathing it in, unable to move as her lungs filled with it.

Karen flinched as Valerie squeezed her arm and gave her a comforting smile. "Hey, at least we're not leaving in handcuffs, right?"

"I guess so," Karen agreed glumly, but she still didn't relish the thought of climbing into the back of that truck again. Her throat felt dry. Already the idea of returning to the truck left her struggling to catch her breath. She'd never suffered from claustrophobia, but the thought of the canvas flap closing behind her made her lightheaded.

"Mommy, are you OK?" Emily looked up and

squeezed Karen's hand a little tighter. "You look sick."

She shook her head, forcing a smile. "I'm fine, honey. Everything's OK."

The officer led them out of the sunlight and into the darkness of the garage, and as they left the light behind Karen felt her pace slow. "There's a gas station about four miles east on highway 20," he said, his voice hollow in the enclosed space. "It should have running water, and they have a store where you can get food. That's as far as I can take you, understand? The 20 is on the main route to the safe zone, so you shouldn't have a problem flagging down a ride."

"That's fine," Ramos replied, flashing Karen a concerned glance. "We appreciate you taking us that far. Ummm... do you mind if Karen rides up front?"

"No, I'm fine," she lied. Her heart was racing so fast she felt as if it was about to burst from her chest.

"You're *not* fine, Karen," Ramos argued. "Seriously, you look terrible. You still need treatment, and the last thing you need right now is any more stress. You can sit up front and get some fresh air." He turned to the officer. "That's OK, right?"

The officer shrugged. "It's fine by me."

Karen smiled gratefully, trying to steady her breathing as they approached the truck. She really didn't want to lose it in front of Emily. She'd already been through enough. "Go on, pumpkin," she said, her voice high and strained. "You can sit in the back with Valerie and the Doc, OK? I'll be right up here with this nice man."

The officer swept back the canvas covering from the back of the truck, and as soon as Karen felt the draft of hot, stale air her head started to swim. She felt as if her throat was closing up. Suddenly she *needed* to get out of the garage more than anything else in the world. She needed fresh air. She needed not to be here, looking up at this truck that just a couple of hours ago she thought would be the last thing she'd ever see.

Without warning – without even realizing what she was doing herself – she turned and ran for the door. Behind her she heard the officer yell out a warning, but his voice was just so much white noise against the ringing in her ears. She couldn't even make out his words, and she didn't care what he was yelling. She just knew she had to get out of there.

By the time she broke out into the sunlight she felt tears streaming down her face. When the warm sun touched her skin she collapsed in a heap on the ground, fighting for air, struggling to take a breath through a throat that felt as if it were being squeezed tight. It only constricted further when the thought flashed through her mind that the soldier's warning could be followed by a gunshot. He could be training his weapon on her right now, squeezing the trigger. At any moment she might feel the bullet tear through her.

Her vision began to narrow to a tunnel. Her breath still failed to come. She knew she'd pass out any second now, and she was terrified that she'd never wake up again. What if the breath didn't come even when she was out cold?

What if this is it? What if this is how I die?

She could barely see anything now. The world was swimming in front of her, the colors faded to muddy grays as her mind began to shut down. All she could see was a shifting blob in front of her, a figure that seemed to crouch at her feet. She felt hands grab her shoulders, but she couldn't tell who it was.

"Deep breaths," a voice called out, loud and clear enough to pierce through the closing fog. "In… and out. In… and out. Feel the air filling your lungs."

She struggled to steal a ragged breath. It wasn't enough.

"It's OK, Karen," the voice assured her. "This is

just temporary. It'll pass. Just focus on your breathing. You're going to be OK. You're safe. You'll get through this."

The voice kept calling out to her calmly, soothing her, encouraging her to breathe until finally, after what felt like an agonizing eternity, she finally managed to drag a full breath down her throat. It washed into her lungs like nectar, thick and nourishing, flooding her blood with oxygen and banishing the washed out gray as her starved brain finally got what it needed. Once the first breath had come the second came a little easier, and then the third, and by the fourth the tight grip had begun to release itself from her throat. She looked up through tear filled eyes, expecting to find Ramos crouching beside her.

It was Krasinski.

"Take your time," he said, patting her on the shoulder before he looked up at something behind her. "Captain, can you hand me your canteen." Behind Karen the officer passed forward a bottle, and Krasinski fished around his jacket pocket until he found a small silver case.

"Here, take this," he said, holding out a pill. Karen took it without thinking, grabbing the canteen and washing it down with a gulp. "It's Xanax," Krasinski said. "It'll help settle you down. I get anxiety attacks too," he explained, before anyone asked. "I could recognize yours a mile away." He watched Karen as she gradually recovered her composure, and when her breathing finally leveled out he took her by the hand and helped her to her feet. "Was that your first attack?"

Karen nodded, wiping tears from her eyes.

"Scariest thing in the world, the first one. Any idea what triggered it?" he asked. "It can be helpful to know the trigger so you're better prepared if it ever happens again."

"It was the truck." Krasinski turned to Emily, pointing into the garage. Her voice trembled as she held back tears. "We were about to get in the truck when she went all white and started breathing funny."

Krasinski looked up at the troop truck, then smiled at Emily. "Thank you, dear. Well, I don't know if this works for you guys, but I think I can help you out with the truck." He took Karen's hand. "How do you think you'd manage in a helicopter?"

"A what?" Karen was sure she'd misheard him.

"A chopper. You're still heading to Truckee, right?" Karen nodded.

"Well, that's where I'm headed now. I managed to hitch a ride on a supply run, and there's plenty of room for you guys if you want to tag along. What do you say?"

The relief was almost enough to make her sob. "I...I'd be OK with it." Karen turned to Ramos and Valerie with hope in her voice. "What do you guys think?"

The two of them exchanged a look, nodding to each other. "Better than waiting at a gas station for a ride," Valerie said. "I say let's go for it. What do you think, Emily?"

Emily looked up at Valerie, surprised to be asked her opinion, and sniffed away a tear. "A helicopter? Is that the one with the whirly thing on top?"

"Yeah, honey, it's got a whirly thing," Karen replied, smiling as she wiped away her own tears. "Do you wanna go for a ride?"

Emily nodded, a grin spreading across her face, her tears forgotten. "Can I sit by the window?"

Karen smiled. "Pumpkin, you can sit by any window you like."

•▼•

CHAPTER SIX
NOT THE SMARTEST MOVE

JACK FELT EVERY muscle in his body tense.

He clutched the steering wheel with both hands, the revolver resting in his lap, and he prayed under his breath as the soldier stepped closer to the car, hoping against hope he wouldn't pull the trigger. Cathy lay face down on the asphalt in front of the car, her hands spread out at her sides.

"I have a gun in here," Jack called out, warning the soldier before he saw it for himself and decided to shoot first and ask questions later. "Revolver on my lap. I'm not touching it, OK? We don't mean you any harm."

The soldier kept his eyes locked on Jack and yelled back to the Humvee. "*Gun!* I need backup. You," he said, addressing Jack again, "how many weapons do you have in the vehicle?"

"Just one," Jack called out. "And Cathy's is on the ground out there. We're not a threat. We don't want anyone to get hurt."

He couldn't take his eyes off the soldier. He looked young, late teens or early twenties, and his inexperience showed. He was panicked, under pressure, and Jack knew the slightest thing might make him do something rash. Even now he could see the soldier's movements become more twitchy and erratic as he waited for help to arrive from the Humvee. His fear was growing by the moment. It was clear that any second now it could boil over.

"Please, sir," he said, fighting to keep his voice steady. "We're not your enemy. Whatever problem we have here let's settle it amicably. I can toss out my gun if it'll make you– "

"*Keep your hands where I can see them!*"

Jack's breath caught in his throat. He hadn't moved an inch, and in the back seat Garside was frozen like a waxwork model.

"OK, OK, we're not moving," he said, deciding that maximum grovelling cooperation might be the only way to save himself from a bullet. "What can we do to help defuse this situation, sir?"

"Both of your step out of the car," the soldier ordered, his voice cracking under stress. "Slowly! Keep your hands where I can see them."

Jack could barely bring himself to move, but after sucking in a deep breath he summoned the nerve to push open his door and climb out, his hands pressed against the roof of the car as he moved with exaggerated care. As he stood the revolver slipped from his lap to the driver's seat, and he raised his hands above the door frame to show that he wasn't a threat.

"*Private! Holster that firearm!*"

The voice calling out from the Humvee was so authoritative, so self assured that as soon as he heard it Jack felt the order go straight to his spine. Without spending so much as a day in the military, the urge to stand to attention was so strong that he almost pulled a muscle fighting it.

Thankfully the young soldier reacted just as strongly. In the blink of an eye calm seemed restored to his world. Those four words seemed to strip him of his fear and panic, restoring in him the absolute certainty that came from the order of a superior officer. He tucked his gun into the holster at his hip and stepped back, his back rod straight. "*Sir, yes sir!*"

A figure climbed down from the back of the Humvee, storming around the side until he finally came into view. He looked around his early fifties, gray hair shorn in a tight crew cut, his uniform failing to hide a small paunch that suggested he spent his days behind a desk rather than on the battlefield. "Now what in the hell's going on here, private? What's the damned hold up?"

The soldier stood so stiffly he looked as if he'd shatter if you pushed him over. "Sir! Three armed civilians in a police patrol car, sir! They fired on us."

"Yeah, I heard the shot." The officer quickly looked Jack up and down before turning back to the young soldier. "OK, stand down before someone ends up dead, y'hear? I told you to warn 'em, not shoot 'em." He turned back to Jack. "Son, you firing at my vehicle?"

Jack froze, unsure how to answer. "Umm... yes, sir. I'm sorry about that. We thought you were someone else."

"Someone else, huh?" He looked back at the white pockmark in the Humvee's windshield. "Well, probably not the smartest move you ever made. A little more firepower and you'd have taken out my driver."

He paused for a moment, pondering what to do next, and then he let out a tired sigh. "But nobody's dead, so today I'm inclined to let it slide." He looked down at Cathy, sprawled out on the road. "Ma'am, you're welcome to stand. Here, lemme help you up." He reached down and offered her a hand, which she took gratefully on the second attempt before shakily climbing to her feet.

"Thank you," she blurted out. "Sorry, I didn't mean to..." She waved a trembling hand to the Humvee. Her face was white as a sheet, and she looked like she was about to burst into tears. "We thought someone was chasing us."

"It's OK, ma'am. We got bigger fish to fry today. Private, can you take this young lady to the truck and get her a drink of water before she falls down?"

The officer turned back to Jack as the private led Cathy away. "I'm Colonel John MacAuliffe," he said, extending a hand. "What's your business here? Where you headed?"

"Jack Archer," he replied. "We're headed for Truckee. We're looking for the safe zone."

The colonel shook his head. "Not a good idea, son. Safe zone ain't safe no more. I'd advise you to turn back the way you came and get yourself on the next road to the east."

Jack felt a chill run down his spine. "What do you mean, it's not safe?"

The colonel shook his head. "I'm sorry, but that's need to know, and you don't need to know. Just believe me when I tell you you don't want to be within a hundred miles of that place. I'm saving your ass. Now turn back and head for highway 36."

"*No!*" Jack was surprised by the force of his own voice. "I'm sorry, I don't mean to yell, but I need to get to Truckee. My wife and daughter are waiting for me there."

The officer's shoulders slumped. "Damn it." He scratched his stubble, eyeballing Jack, weighing up the pros and cons of giving away classified information. Eventually he gave up with a sigh. "Son, I'm afraid I have some bad news. You might want to take a seat for this."

Jack shook his head. "I'll stand. What happened?"

MacAuliffe reached into his breast pocket and pulled out a half smoked cigar, rolling it between his fingers as he spoke. "My men and I came from the Truckee camp just a couple hours ago. We're on a pharmacy run, gathering supplies from the towns up here, but ten minutes ago we received new orders to regroup at Beale AFB. The camp's being evacuated."

Jack felt his breath catch in his throat. He leaned back against the hood of the cruiser, his knees suddenly weak. "Evacuated? Why?"

The colonel took a deep breath, and his face creased into a frown. "This is classified, but… hell, if you got skin in the game I guess you deserve to know what's going on." He placed his hand on Jack's shoulder and leaned in. "There's gonna be another attack. A bomb was found on one of the supply trucks coming in to the camp, and we believe the intention is to destroy the safe zone." He pointed back the way they'd come. "You're damned lucky we spotted you. We were about to head west to Marysville when we saw you back at that last junction. Who knows what you'd be driving into if we hadn't caught up with you."

"When you say bomb, do you mean…?"

MacAuliffe nodded. "It's nuclear, yes."

Hearing the colonel's words Jack felt the bottom fall out of his world. *He was so close.* Karen and Emily were just a few dozen miles away. He could almost feel them in his arms, and now… now they were being snatched away in the cruelest way imaginable.

"The evacuation," he asked. "It's going on now? Will they get everyone out in time?"

"I'm sorry, son, but I just don't know. We've been trying to get the camp back on comms since we heard. All I know is that there were around seventy thousand civilians at the camp by the time we left, and more were arriving by the minute. That's a hell of a lot of people to evacuate on short notice, but we just have to keep our fingers crossed."

"Colonel!" The private ran back from the Humvee holding an over-sized field radio. "We've raised Truckee. I have Captain Standish on the line for you."

"Hot damn," MacAuliffe said, chewing on his cigar as he grabbed the radio in both hands. "Standish? I hope you have some news for me, 'cause you know I don't like sitting here in the dark."

The radio crackled, and a faint voice drifted in over a deep rumble emanating from the speaker. "Yes, sir. The serial number matches item eight on the itinerary. You were right, sir, it's part of the Incirlik arsenal. The boys tell me this one is… hang on, I wrote it on my hand… it's a W80 dialed in for five kilotons. It's been activated, and they tell me that the command disable mechanism has been tampered with. They said it's been set up for the conventional payload to detonate if they so much as show it a screwdriver. Whoever screwed with this thing sure knew what they were doing, sir."

MacAuliffe cursed under his breath. "OK, what's going on now? Are they getting everyone out OK?"

The radio crackled again, as if the man on the other end was holding the transmit key, but for a long moment there was only the deep rumble in the background. Finally, just as MacAuliffe raised the radio to speak again, the voice returned.

"Well I'm... I guess I'm around five miles east of Carpenter Ridge right now, sir. They told me the further north the better if we want to keep the fallout from hitting Reno."

MacAuliffe frowned. "Say again, Captain. I'm not sure I'm reading you."

"There's an old gold mine close to Hobart Mills, sir. I figure if I can get it deep enough into the shaft it might contain some of the blast."

The colonel's face turned white. The cigar fell from his lips as his jaw fell slack. "Standish, are you saying you have the nuke with you?"

"Yes, sir," came the quiet reply. "I'm sorry, sir.

There was no way we could get everyone out in time."

MacAuliffe stabbed at the air with a finger as he spoke. "Captain, stop that truck right now! Get out and run south. If you leave now you can still clear the blast radius!"

A long silence, followed by a quiet voice. "I'm sorry, sir, but no. Here's the turnoff for Hobart Mills."

"Standish, I'm giving you a direct order. Get out of the truck. You're already out of range of the camp. You hear me? *Get out of the God damned truck!*"

There was no response.

The colonel yelled into the radio again, unleashing a string of curses at the captain, but it was hopeless. He called impotently into the radio for minutes, but the louder he demanded that Standish run away the more insistently the ensuing silence sounded the captain's refusal. It was clear he wasn't going to reply. MacAuliffe was trying to give orders to a man who had already accepted his fate.

"*God damn it!*" The colonel yelled, hammering his fist against the hood of the cruiser. He spun on his heels, desperately searching for something, *anything*, he could do to prevent what he knew was about to happen.

Finally MacAuliffe's shoulders slumped. He dropped the radio at his feet, staring south across the endless pine forest. He knew there was nothing he could do to save Standish. The die had been cast. All he could do now was–

The silent flash appeared on the horizon.

Jack threw himself to the ground.

•▼•

CHAPTER SEVEN
BRACE

"DID YOU KNOW I've never been on a helicopter?"

Valerie smiled down at Emily, a broad smile beaming out from beneath a set of ear protectors so large they covered her cheeks. "You know what?" She leaned in and whispered conspiratorially. "Neither have I."

Emily raised her eyebrows with surprise. "Really? Never ever?"

"No, honey, never ever *ever*," Valerie laughed. "I think most of the people who ride helicopters are soldiers and people with a lot of money. Bus drivers like me don't really get the chance."

"Have you ever been on a airplane?" Emily asked, and then continued before Valerie could open her mouth to answer. "I go on the airplane to see grandma in Texas. We went in the summer. She has a new dog to play with."

"Oh wow, that's great! Do you– "

"His name's Custard," she interrupted, "because he's yellow like custard."

In the seat beside Valerie Ramos groaned, his eyes closed and head hanging between his knees.

"What's wrong with Doctor Ramos?" Emily asked.

"I don't think he likes to fly," whispered Valerie. "I think it makes him feel a little sick."

"*Mmmm hmmm,*" Ramos muttered, leaning back. He forced his eyes open as a gassy belch bubbled up his throat. "Honey," he said, looking down at Emily, "do you think we could have a little quiet time? I'm not feeling great, and the noise is…" He trailed off and waved a hand as another belch arrived.

Emily pursed her lips and nodded. She turned and sat back in her seat by the window, and for a few moments she gazed out at the arid landscape far below. She looked distracted, as if she were counting in her head, and after ten seconds she turned back to Valerie. "You know Custard isn't really *made* of custard. He's a real dog. He's just the same color as custard."

Another few seconds of silence passed.

"Do you like custard?"

Karen swooped in and grabbed Emily beneath her arms as Ramos began to groan again.

"Hey, pumpkin," she said, planting the little girl on her lap. "We have to be extra quiet, OK? Just until we land."

"But I'm *excited*, mommy! I've never been in a helicopter."

"I know, pumpkin," Karen replied, stroking her hair. "I heard you the first five times."

"Have you ever been in a helicopter, mommy?" Emily tugged at Karen's shirt. "*Mommy.* Did you hear me? I said have you ever been in a helicopter?"

"Hold on, honey," Karen replied, brushing her off as she peered out the window. "Where are these guys going? Ted? *Hey, Ted!*"

Krasinski turned back to face the cabin from his seat beside the pilot, shaking his head and tapping his ear protectors. "I can't hear you. What is it?"

"Stay here, honey," Karen told Emily, planting her firmly in her seat. "I'll be right back." She walked in a stooped crouch towards the cockpit and leaned over the back of the pilot's seat. "What's going on down there?" she asked, pointing out the window.

Krasinski frowned. "What do you mean?"

"The trucks. Look down there," she said. "There's a huge convoy on the highway, heading west. Is that your guys?"

Krasinski craned his neck, peering down at the ground below. "Where the hell are they going?" he muttered. A seemingly endless train of cars and trucks crowded the black ribbon of asphalt, a slow moving snake that stretched so far that its tail was lost in the haze. "I don't know why our people would be moving west *en masse*. There's nothing in that direction apart from Beale." He tapped the pilot on the arm. "Hey, can you get Delta on the horn? Ask them what's happening down on the highway."

Karen watched the pilot as he called into his mic in a crisp tone, and after a few seconds of silence she jumped with surprise when the urgent response came through loud and clear, ringing out of the headphones she'd assumed were just sound canceling mufflers.

"What's your location?" The voice brusquely demanded, almost drowned out by yelling in the background. The pilot calmly read out a long string of coordinates, and when the response came back it was so loud Karen had to pull the headphones away from her ears.

"Get out of there, *now!* Withdraw at max speed, and brace for turbulence!"

The pilot didn't need a second warning. He tugged back sharply on the yoke, pulling the Huey into a sudden steep, banking climb that sent Karen tumbling backwards. In the blink of an eye the floor of the chopper became a wall. She reached out and clutched at the pilot's seat with grasping fingers, but it all happened too quickly. She couldn't get a grip. As the Huey climbed she fell back through the cabin, landing painfully shoulder first against a steel bulkhead above the seats.

Karen looked around, dazed and disoriented. Ramos and Valerie braced against each other as they were pressed down hard into their seats, jaws clenched and eyes closed, too afraid to scream out. Emily did the screaming for all of them. She hadn't been buckled into her seat, and now she was pressed against the rear wall, clinging to Valerie's shoulder as the shifting G force tossed her back and forth. One moment she was pinned against the seats, and the next she was tossed like a rag doll against the sliding door of the side wall.

As the Huey turned into a sharp bank she tumbled

sideways once again, but this time Karen was ready for her. She wrapped one arm in the black webbing that ran along the cabin's rear wall, and as Emily fell away from the side door Karen launched herself out into open space, reaching out to grab hold of her daughter as she tumbled by.

Emily crumpled over her mother's arm, the wind knocked out of her by the impact, but as soon as she realized Karen had a hold on her she clutched at the arm like a spider monkey clinging to its mother, wrapping her arms tight around her, refusing to let go.

"*I've got you!*" Karen gasped as she pulled Emily in closer, but there was no way she could hear her over the roar of the engine and the klaxons wailing from the cockpit.

"*Mommy!*" Emily screamed, wide eyed. Karen could only see her lips move.

And then the world turned a blinding white.

•▼•

CHAPTER EIGHT
ONE LAST LOOK AT THE SUN

CAPTAIN JAMES STANDISH dropped his radio to the bench seat of the truck, turning his attention back to the road. MacAuliffe's voice continued to call out angrily from the seat, but Standish blocked it out. He needed to concentrate. He didn't know these roads. The only directions he had were those he'd been able to memorize after a quick scan of a map back at safe zone Delta.

He almost missed the turnoff from highway 89 when he reached it. It was little more than a dusty track, unpaved and overgrown, visible only by a narrow break in the pine forest. Standish had been expecting something a little better marked, but he figured it made sense. Hobart Mills itself had been abandoned since the 1930s, and the gold mine long before that, but the map still detailed the entrance to the shaft along with an old trail where the spoil had been carried out in carts. There was no earthly reason for it to be paved.

He spun the wheel and sent the truck crawling into the forest, worrying for a moment that it would be too wide to fit between the trees that had overtaken the old mill town. It was clear no vehicles had passed this way in years, but Standish was determined to force his way through, and he had the saving grace of knowing he'd never be held to account for damaging military property. This was a one way trip. He'd taken his last order.

Standish barreled into the young, spindly pines that lined the track with all the speed he could muster, splintering their trunks and whipping aside branches as he forced the truck through the tight gap. A couple of the trees fought back against the attack, hammering the front of the truck before giving up the struggle, and after just a minute or so the windshield was already cracked in several places. Steam rose from the hood, probably from a busted radiator, and Standish knew he'd have to push on before the engine gave up the ghost.

Three hundred yards. That's how far the map had told him he'd need to drive before the old mining trail would come into view on his left, but the closer he came the more he worried he'd never find it. The forest was just too overgrown. There were no gaps in the trees wide enough to force his way through. Hell, maybe the map was wrong. Maybe this hadn't been the right turnoff after all. Maybe the entrance to the mine was a mile away, on the other side of centuries old forest.

Wait.

There it was. Almost invisible, hidden by decades of growth, he could make out a path weaving through the forest fifty yards to the north. Even from here he could see the old lumber that framed the entrance to the mine, almost petrified by years of exposure to the cold mountain air.

"*Come on come on come on,*" he whispered under his breath as he swung the wheel and shifted down a gear, turning the lumbering truck onto the rocky path through the trees. He swore as the truck bounced, struggling for grip on the loose gravel, and he winced at the sound of the missile crashing around the back. He knew it would brush off rough treatment like this – the W80's casing was designed to survive the violence of a launch without accidental detonation – but still he clenched his teeth at the sound of it sliding from wall to wall.

The mouth of the mine was just a few dozen yards away now. Through the trees Standish could see the rotting boards hammered across the front, and he turned the truck squarely at the center of the entrance and stepped on the gas. With a silent prayer he took one last look at the sun, and then he let out a determined roar as he plunged into the mine.

The truck broke through the boards as easily as if they were a mist. With a great crash and the ear splitting screech of steel on rock the truck plowed into the pitch blackness beyond the shaft entrance. Standish kept his foot on the gas, driving blind, desperate to forge ahead as far as he could go. Every yard was priceless. Every extra inch might save another hundred lives.

Five seconds passed, and then ten. He was still going. He had no idea how deep he was. He could only tell the truck was still moving by the rattling vibrations. There was no frame of reference, not a hint of light in the blackness, and Standish had forgotten to switch on the headlights before he crashed through the entrance.

All he knew was that he was still moving forward, and the roar of the engine echoing back at him told him that the passage was narrowing ahead of him. The walls were closing in. Through the open window it sounded like they were just inches away, and after a few seconds the truck hit something immovable. It stopped dead, but Standish didn't. He jolted forward and slammed his forehead against the windshield before slumping back, dazed, into the sprung seat.

The captain was struck dumb by the pain. He'd bitten his tongue as he hit the glass, and already he could taste the coppery blood in his mouth. His head swam. He could feel more blood running from his forehead and into his right eye, but his left was still clear. With a searching hand he fumbled blindly across the dash for the headlight switch, and when he finally found it a single bulb cast its light through the dusty darkness ahead.

It was a solid wall. The shaft stopped dead six inches ahead of the hood. To the left and right it branched off, but both passages were far too narrow for the truck even if he could somehow maneuver it into one of them. This was as far as it would ever go.

Standish used his sleeve to wipe the blood from his eye, and as he looked out at the wall ahead he was gripped by an overwhelming feeling of relief. He had no idea how deep into the shaft he'd driven. He had no clue if it would change anything, if it was enough to protect a single person from the force of the blast, but he knew he'd given everything he had. He knew he hadn't wimped out at the last minute. He'd driven until he was stopped by solid rock. Nobody could say he hadn't done the uniform proud.

Now, though... now he felt as if he were waking up from a dream. He looked around at the cab of the truck, the cab he'd assumed would be his last resting place, and he suddenly realized it didn't have to be that way. He was free now. He'd taken the bomb as far as he could. For all he knew it was set on a timer to detonate an hour from now. It could be set to go off a *week* from now, or maybe there wasn't a timer at all. There was no reason he had to just sit around and wait for it to explode.

I don't have to die. I can survive this.

With a rush of exhilaration he reached over to the door and pushed it open. At first it didn't want to budge – the crash had buckled the frame – but when he put his shoulder to it he managed to force just enough of a gap to slide out, emptying his lungs to squeeze painfully through the narrow opening.

The stale air of the mine caught at the back of his throat. His arrival had kicked up the thick layer of dust that had settled over a century of silent darkness, and now it stung at his eyes. He could barely breathe. In the near darkness through scratchy, tear filled eyes he could barely see, but he didn't let it slow him down. He picked his way along the narrow gap between the truck and the stone wall, and when he finally reached the tailgate he saw a dim shaft of sunlight picked out in the floating dust, maybe thirty yards behind the truck.

"*Shit*," he cursed under his breath, feeling his way along the shaft back towards the surface. He'd hoped he'd made it further than thirty yards. It felt as if he'd driven much deeper, but he felt no shame. He'd taken it as far as he could.

Standish stumbled painfully over rocks as he picked his way through the half light. With each step the blackness was banished a little more, but it still wasn't enough to guide the way. All the dim light did was cast an edge to the darkness. He saw the outlines of the rock face but still the jagged edges poked at his legs, and loose spoil still threatened to turn his ankles.

He climbed for what felt like hours, though he knew it was only a couple of minutes. Time seemed to pass more slowly in the terrifying blackness, and by the time he made it back to the entrance he felt as if he hadn't taken a full breath in an eternity. His lungs felt parched, his throat choked with dust, and he scrambled on hands and knees half expecting to collapse just out of reach of the sunlight.

But no. With a joyous cry he finally broke into the shaft of light. He laughed, clambering more quickly across the shattered boards at the entrance, and with a triumphant yell he tumbled back into the bright daylight. He coughed, spitting out a mouthful of dust and blinking away tears, and finally he managed to drink down a deep breath of fresh, crisp pine-scented air.

For a long moment Standish stayed at the entrance on hands and knees, greedily sucking down breaths of the clean air. He knew time may not be on his side but he needed to gather himself. For a moment he needed to simply *exist*, to realize that he was there, *alive*, in the light of God's creation.

And then he broke into a run.

Standish knew the bomb was small, at least in relation to most in the nuclear arsenal. It was a tactical weapon set with a yield of just five kilotons, even less than the destructive force of the bomb dropped on Hiroshima. This wasn't a city killer. It was survivable. The fireball would only reach a few hundred meters from the blast, and if he could make it a mile he'd probably avoid serious burns. Two miles from the blast and if he was lucky he might even get away with only minor injuries.

The dirt track stretched out ahead of him, leading him back to the road where he could turn south. He'd be able to sprint once he reached the asphalt. On level ground he could cover a couple of miles in… what, fifteen minutes? He could make it. He just wished he'd grabbed his radio from the seat before he'd left the truck. It would be much easier if he could–

He didn't get the chance to finish the thought.

For a brief instant the mountainside *blurred*. As the bomb detonated beneath a few dozen yards of solid rock the earth fought back for a moment, mounting a vain defense against the power of the blast, and the forest trembled before it was overwhelmed. A moment later it vanished, vaporized, and the collapsing mountainside was lost in the blinding light of the fireball.

The shock wave raced out across the landscape, flattening pines in their tens of thousands in an expanding circle that reached a mile from the epicenter in just a couple of seconds. Beyond that the trees bent so low that their tops almost touched the ground, but as the wave passed they bounced back with the deafening sound of a million gunshots.

The convoy from safe zone Delta stretched five miles from end to end. Those at its head saw the shock wave pass by as a ripple spreading out across the world, a rolling wave that shook the trees and lifted the trucks on their suspension coils for a moment. The trucks at the rear, on the other hand…

The roaring gale from the epicenter tossed two dozen trucks into the air like toys, tumbling them end on end, hurling their passengers out to fall to the ground below. Just a few hundred meters further along the convoy the trucks barely trembled, but the cruel hand of fate picked out two hundred or more men, women and children. It chose the last of the evacuees, those who'd lingered when the evacuation was called, and it punished their tardiness with death.

As the shock wave passed the tail end of the convoy, far above it fate turned its attention to the Huey…

•▼•

CHAPTER NINE
A LEAF ON THE WIND

NOBODY ABOARD THE chopper saw the explosion. They were already facing back towards Beale by the time the flash appeared on the horizon, but there was no mistaking what was happening. The flash flooded through every window, replacing the world outside with a blinding, terrifying light. For a moment the engine roar and the cockpit alarms seemed to fade into the background, replaced by the cloying, expectant silence before the sound of the blast reached them.

Karen knew what was coming. She'd been here before, and in the few seconds of eerie calm that passed between the flash and the shock wave she convinced herself that she was prepared for its violence. She told herself that the second time wouldn't be quite so bad, stripped of the element of surprise. She'd survived this once before, and she could do it again.

She wrapped her arm tighter into the webbing, and with her other arm she squeezed Emily so tight she could feel her ribs flex. So tight that the little girl gasped with pain, but Karen knew she couldn't loosen her grip.

"*Brace!*"

Karen looked around the cabin, eyes wide with terror, and for a moment time seemed to stop. The blinding flash seemed to freeze the world in a terrifying *tableau vivant*. In the cockpit the pilot gripped the yoke for dear life, steeling himself for a shock that would toss the Huey as easily as a dandelion seed in a gale, clinging to the stick as if he could possibly keep the craft under control in its wake. Valerie and Ramos clutched each other arm in arm, eyes tightly closed and heads bowed in the brace position. Krasinski pressed his face against the window, staring down in horror as the first of the trucks were lifted from the ground and torn apart. When the wave finally hit he was halfway through crossing himself, his mouth open in prayer.

It only took a second for Karen to realize she was wrong. The second time was no easier. The terror was sharper now *because* she knew what was coming. She knew exactly how much it would hurt, and she knew the chances of surviving a second blast were vanishingly small. She clenched her teeth and waited for the end to come.

The violent turbulence of the shock wave spun the chopper end on end, the G force tearing Karen away from the webbing and trying to steal Emily from her arms. She wanted to scream, but she couldn't make a sound as the helicopter locked into its wild spin. She couldn't even take a breath, the weight on her chest was so heavy. The deafening roar of the blast felt like a physical presence squeezing her skull, but she couldn't free her hands to cover her ears.

"We're going down!" The pilot's panicked voice was almost silent as he called over the deafening roar, and a cloud of thick black smoke billowed from the rotor. Somewhere above them something snapped. Karen couldn't hear it, but she felt the jolt through her body, a jolt that told her that something very important had gone badly wrong. The chopper shivered in mid air, and seconds later a steel panel buckled and collapsed from the ceiling. A shower of greasy oil sprayed down from a severed hose, and in the blink of an eye the smoke was in the cabin, choking her. Blinding her. The smell of burning plastic and searing oil caught in her throat, stealing what little breath she had.

Now Karen could barely hear the pilot over the screaming alarms in the cockpit, but she saw the fear in his eyes as he hollered into the radio. "Mayday, mayday, mayday! Alpha Foxtrot seven five one nine two! Engine failure, executing a controlled descent from eleven hundred feet at…" he looked out the window with a terrified expression. "Two miles south of Spaulding Lake!"

With a tremendous effort he hauled at the stick, fighting the G force that tried to squeeze him against the window, and somehow he managed to pull the Huey out of its spin. The invisible hand that pressed Karen against the bulkhead suddenly released its grip. She tumbled to the ground, and as she untangled her arm from the webbing she desperately hauled Emily back into her seat.

"*Strap her in!*" she yelled to Valerie, but just as she got a grip on Emily's belt a new alarm began to sound from the cockpit, joining the cacophony. The engine let out a high pitched whine that grew more urgent by the second until it sounded as if something were about to explode, but just as the whine felt set to peak there was a cough, a sputter, and the engine died.

The Huey began to fall from the sky.

Karen's stomach flipped over as she was lifted back towards the ceiling. Her feet left the ground, but she refused to release her grip on the seatbelt. Valerie held one hand across Emily's chest, pinning her to her seat as Karen desperately fumbled with the belt. In the cockpit the pilot let out a primal roar, pulling back with all his strength on the stick, and Karen screamed as the chopper swooped out of its dive, sending her crashing back down to the floor.

She ignored the pain. She didn't have time to worry about it. She grabbed the belt once more, struggling to mate the ends in the chaos, and finally she felt it click into place just as the Huey plunged down once again. Emily reached up for her mom's hand as Karen was torn away, but she couldn't reach it.

Karen slammed face first against the side door. She couldn't see a thing, but somehow she managed to find a section of webbing with blindly searching hands, and she clung on for dear life as she blinked away the tears.

Now she could see out the window. She didn't want to. The last thing she wanted to remember was that they were high in the air without an engine, but she had no choice. Her face was pressed against the glass, and with her eyes wide with terror she was forced to look down at the ground below. The convoy was in disarray. Dozens of trucks were overturned. A few more were in pieces, the flaming debris scattered across the elevated highway and into the forest beneath it.

The Huey was only a few hundred feet above the ground now, and it was clear the pilot was trying to guide the stricken craft towards the black ribbon of asphalt. It looked like the only landing site for miles around, the only level ground within reach, but even as the chopper descended toward it Karen could see that it wouldn't be easy. The road wasn't clear. Hundreds of cars and trucks still crowded the asphalt and now, with the immense mushroom cloud climbing into the sky behind them, hundreds of passengers had climbed out from their ruined vehicles to watch the spectacle, or flee from it. The road was teeming with people, vehicles and debris, and the pilot clearly didn't have the control needed for a precision landing.

"*We're coming in!*" he yelled, gritting his teeth as the road loomed up beneath them. Just a hundred feet now, close enough to see the faces of the people. Seventy feet, and the crowds on the highway began to scatter in all directions, fleeing the chopper as it tumbled from the sky. Fifty, then forty, thirty, twenty, and now the chaos was complete. One of the drivers in the convoy tried to gun his canvas-topped troop truck past the stalled line. He veered out into the road and stepped on the gas, sounding his horn to clear a path as the vehicle straddled the shoulder and scraped along the concrete barrier.

The pilot tried to react, but it was too late. The controls were sluggish in his hands. All he could do was slow their descent, but he couldn't alter their direction. The Huey was coming down directly into the path of the truck, and it seemed the driver hadn't noticed them at all.

"Hold on to something!" the pilot yelled out, unnecessarily. Through the window Karen saw the truck suddenly swerve as the driver finally caught sight of the chopper looming above him. He turned into another truck, scraping against its side, and one of the Huey's landing skids caught the edge of the canvas roof.

The pilot tugged back on the yoke and sent the chopper reeling back away from the highway, tearing the roof from the truck as the Huey careened backwards. A dozen terrified passengers looked up through the torn roof, falling to the floor as the edge of the rotor caught on the steel frame. The Huey span, thrown away from the truck by the glancing blow, and Karen clenched her teeth and squeezed closed her eyes as the skids crashed down onto the concrete crash barrier beside the road.

For a moment nobody dared to breathe. Nobody dared move. Nobody spoke.

The landing skids of the Huey were resting on the four foot high concrete crash barrier at the edge of the elevated highway. The rotor was still lazily spinning, tilting the chopper back and forth as it tried to find its balance. It was as if gravity was still making up its mind in which direction to push the craft. Forward to a soft landing on the asphalt, or backwards to the forest floor far below.

"I…" The pilot slowly turned in his seat. "I think the tail rotor's caught on something." Slowly, carefully he unclipped his harness, and with glacial speed he climbed out of his seat and gently cracked open his door. "Nobody move," he muttered, poking his head out for a moment. When he returned his face was drained of its color.

"OK," he mumbled, eyes wide. "OK... You, big guy," he said, pointing to Ramos. "I need you to slowly move forward to the cockpit. No sudden movements, OK?"

Ramos shook his head. "Get the girl out first. I'm not leaving her behind."

The pilot took a deep breath, forcing himself to remain calm. "Sir, I need you to listen carefully. I don't want you to panic, but the only thing keeping us from falling back right now is the edge of the tail rotor resting on a tree." He pointed above his head. "Right now the main rotor is still spinning, spreading our weight evenly from back to front, but as soon as it comes to rest it could tip the balance towards the back, and then we'll be screwed. You're the heaviest guy in the chopper, sir. I need you up here to help tip the balance, you understand?"

Ramos reluctantly nodded, unclipping his seatbelt. Emily began to cry as he slowly rose from the seat, reaching out for him.

"Pumpkin, *no!*" Karen warned, her voice harsher than she'd intended. Emily froze, shocked by her tone, and Karen had to fight the unbearable urge to rush to her and wrap her in a hug. "Let the doctor go, OK? We'll join him in just a second, I promise."

"It's OK, honey," Ramos assured her. "You and your mom will come soon. Just wait there, OK?" With a deep breath he took a faltering step towards the front, his back hunched beneath the low ceiling. Another step, and this time there came an ominous creak.

"*Stop!*"

Ramos froze, and a moment later another creak sounded. Above them the whir of the freewheeling rotor was beginning to slow, and beneath her feet Karen could feel the fuselage tremble. Something was going to give.

"OK, forward slowly," the pilot ordered, failing to keep the panic from his voice as Ramos reached the cockpit and stepped between the seats. "Now you." He pointed to Valerie. "A little quicker, OK?"

Valerie didn't need to be told twice. Her belt was already unbuckled, and she covered the distance across the cabin in three steps. She joined Ramos and Krasinski beside the crowded passenger seat, each of them ready to dive for the door at a moment's notice.

The rotor was noticeably slower now. Through the

window Karen could now pick out individual blades as it slowed from a blur.

"Now pass me the girl," the pilot ordered, holding out his arms.

Karen reached back to unbuckle Emily from her seat. "It's OK, pumpkin," she whispered soothingly. "We'll be outside in just a minute. We just have to…"

Her voice trailed off as another deep, tortured groan sounded, this time from the back of the chopper. Above her the rotor slowed to a lazy spin, one full turn every few seconds, and Karen could feel what was happening through her shoes. The chopper was tilting back. The movement was too slight to see, just a fraction of a degree, but her inner ear couldn't be fooled. She knew it, and from the look in his eyes the pilot knew it too. He froze.

"The door," he said, shifting his eyes to point at the door beside her. "You have to jump for it."

Karen shook her head. "I… I can't."

The pilot nodded. "You can. There's no choice. We only have a few seconds. See the door handle by your left hand?"

Karen didn't dare move her head. She held her breath as she turned her eyes to the handle. "Uh huh."

"Pull that straight back towards you, and when you hear the click you have to push it away from you. The door will swing right out. The road is right outside the door, OK? All you have to do is jump."

Another long creak. Now the rotor was almost still. Karen felt tears run down her cheeks and panic grip at her throat. Her legs felt frozen in place. "I can't jump," she cried, her voice barely a whisper.

"*If you don't jump Emily will die.*"

That was Valerie. She spoke matter-of-factually. No emotion. No panic. No yelling. Just a simple, undeniable promise of what would happen to her daughter if Karen failed to act. If she couldn't overcome her fear she'd be killing Emily. It was as coldly simple as that.

The tough love worked. As the rotor spun to a stop above her Karen found herself able to move again. She reached out and took the handle. "OK. OK, I can do it."

The pilot nodded. "On three, everyone jumps. Guys, you ready?" A murmur from behind him assured him that the others were on board. "OK, one... two... *three!*"

Karen pushed open the door, and as it swung back

on its hinges she felt the floor shift beneath her. The Huey was tipping backwards as gravity finally noticed it had unfinished business. With one arm she scooped Emily from her seat by the door, and she held the other protectively ahead of her as she stumbled gracelessly out onto the asphalt six feet below her. She fell into a clumsy roll, scrambling away from the stricken chopper as it fell backwards. With a squeal of terror she turned and looked back, and her heart froze as she saw what was happening.

They weren't moving quickly enough. Krasinski jumped down first, followed closely by Ramos, but on the other side of the chopper it looked like Valerie was struggling to reach the door. She was thrown off balance as the chopper tilted back, hurling her back into the pilot's seat.

"*Go!*" Behind her the pilot yelled, climbing between the seats and back into the cockpit. It all happened in just a few seconds, but Karen watched as the pilot looked at the wide open door the others had jumped through. He could easily make it. Just a couple of steps and he'd be free. He'd be safe.

But then he turned away and grabbed Valerie. With the strength lent to him by fear and panic he took her by the collar and lifted her from the seat, and with an almighty shove he tossed her out the door, pushing himself back into the chopper in the process. Valerie hit the asphalt on her hands and knees, dazed and confused.

The fuselage tipped beyond the point of no return. As it tilted the pilot fell away from the cockpit, vanishing into the back. The rotor scythed through the treetops as it fell, and the nose vanished over the edge of the highway and plunged to the forest floor a hundred feet below.

There was no explosion. No spectacular fireworks. There was only an almighty crash as the fuselage crumpled on impact, and as Karen stumbled to the edge and peered over she caught the first flicker of flames catching at the oil that coated the inside of the craft. It only took a few seconds to catch, and before long it was a roaring inferno. There was no hint of movement from within.

The pilot was gone.

•▼•

CHAPTER TEN

WHY DIAL THEM DOWN?

ALL WAS SILENT in the Humvee as it chewed through the miles of winding mountain road.

Nobody felt like talking, not while the mushroom cloud still loomed over them through the dust-shrouded rear window, and Jack more than most was happy to just sit quietly. He was in no mood to chat while Karen and Emily's fate hung in the air, a question mark that dwarfed even the cloud.

Things had moved quickly after the flash had faded. Colonel MacAuliffe hadn't allowed himself much time to mourn the loss of his captain. As soon as the swiftly weakening shock wave passed them by and the distant rumble began to die away he'd picked himself up and paced back and forth for a few seconds, swearing under his breath even as the mushroom cloud billowed far above them, but then he'd found a degree of self control Jack could only admire. One deep breath was all it took before the emotion vanished from his face, and he once again became the commander his men needed him to be.

There were three men in the colonel's squad. Jack had already seen the driver and the young private, but a third had emerged from the back of the Humvee and, on the colonel's orders, plucked Jack's keys from his hand. In just a few minutes he and the private had transferred the pharmacy supplies they'd been gathering into the trunk of the cruiser, and with a curt salute they'd climbed in and departed for the north to continue their scavenging duties.

It hadn't occurred to Jack to complain, to argue that it was *his* car. He got the impression the colonel wasn't in the mood to listen.

Now Jack sat crowded in the back of the Humvee with Cathy, Garside and Boomer, nervously gnawing at a thumbnail as he stared out the windshield, scanning the road ahead for signs for the Air Force base. His foot subconsciously pressed into the floor as if he were stepping on the gas pedal, urging the Humvee to move faster.

At least *part* of him wanted to move faster.

He didn't want to give voice to his fears, but part of him was terrified about arriving at Beale. He tried to force the thoughts from his mind, but they easily slipped past his defenses.

What if he reached the base and learned the girls hadn't made it? What if – he felt his heart thump in his chest – what if he got there and found only Karen, or just Emily? What if one of them had been caught in the blast? What if they'd been separated, and Emily was stranded back in the fallout zone? What if they'd been evacuated in the wrong direction, and they were now headed for Reno on the wrong side of the irradiated landscape? What if, what if, what if–

"*Stop it!*"

Jack jumped at the sound of his own voice. It took him a moment to realize it even *was* his voice.

"You OK, Jack?" Cathy asked, squeezing his shoulder.

He shrugged her away, not unkindly but a little roughly.

"Yeah. Yeah, I'm fine. I'm just…" He pushed himself from his seat and shuffled forward, bent double until he reached the front seats. "Colonel, how long before we get to the base?"

MacAuliffe looked up from a stack of papers in his lap. "Hmm?" He glanced at his watch. "Oh, about a half hour, provided the roads stay clear." He turned his attention back to his papers, muttering under his breath, and within moments he seemed to forget that Jack was there. "Just doesn't make any God damn sense," he whispered to himself, tapping his pen on the topmost sheet.

Jack couldn't resist sneaking a look. He peered over the colonel's shoulder and saw that it was a list, the handwritten scrawl almost impossible to read. Jack could only make out that the top of the list read 9 x W80, and beside the list in red ink were four words.

Why dial them down?

"I'm sorry, can I help you with something?"

Jack looked up to find the colonel glaring over his shoulder at him.

"I..." he babbled, feeling his face flush pink, "I'm sorry, I didn't mean to..."

"These are classified documents, son," MacAuliffe scolded, turning the papers over to prevent Jack from reading them. "You shouldn't be prying."

"I'm sorry, I was just curious," he said, settling in the seat behind the driver. The colonel scowled and returned to the papers, and for a moment Jack remained silent before he came to a decision. *Oh, what the hell.* It's not like the colonel would arrest him for asking a question.

"Are they the nukes?" he asked, nodding to the list and bracing himself for a dressing down.

"Jack," MacAuliffe turned back to him impatiently, "do you not understand the meaning of the word classified?"

"I know, I know, it's just… well, I heard the captain on the radio say something about a W80, and I see the same code on that list. He said it was one of the items on the itinerary, right?"

He paused for a moment, hoping he wasn't overstepping the mark by too much. "I guess I'm just wondering how you have a list of the different types of bombs. Did… did you guys know these things were out there before the attacks?"

MacAuliffe stared at him in silence for a beat too long for comfort, so long that Jack felt like a bug under a magnifying glass, just waiting for it to shift and focus a beam of sunlight on him. He felt sweat prickle at his collar, and just as he was about to give up and retreat to the safety of Cathy and Garside the colonel seemed to reach a decision.

"Oh, what the hell," he sighed, his shoulders slumped. He passed the sheet back towards Jack. "It's not like we'll be able to keep any of this a secret much longer. Yeah, these are the nukes."

"Sir?" The driver glanced sidelong at the colonel, speaking in a tone as firm as he dared use with a superior officer. "I have to remind you that these documents are code word protected, and I don't have the clearance to know their contents. Are you sure it's a good idea to– "

MacAuliffe raised a hand to silence him.

"Your objection is noted, Lieutenant, but I need fresh eyes on this. I won't hold it against you if you feel the need to report the breach, and if you don't want to be involved you can feel free to pull over and step outside for a minute. Sounds fair?"

"Understood, sir," the driver reluctantly nodded. "I'll stay. I just want my protest on record."

The colonel gave him an amused half smile. "I'll be sure to note it down when this is all over, Lieutenant." He turned back to Jack, who was peering at the list in an attempt to understand the chicken scratch. Eight of the lines had red pen notations beside them, each the name of a city.

9 x W80

Nakharov – 20-30kt – San Diego intended target?
Jian Sing – 5kt – Los Angeles
Al-Shuyoukh – 5kt - Bakersfield
Madain Saleh – 5kt – Fresno
Novoyepalatinsk – 5kt – Sacramento
Qingdao III – 5kt – San Francisco
Faisal Raj – 150kt – Portland
10kt – Truckee
W80 – ?

"So what am I looking at, exactly? I don't know all that much about nukes. Am I looking at nine bombs here?"

MacAuliffe nodded. "Altogether, yeah. Nine W80 tactical warheads. Our satellite intel tells us that they were mounted on modified MGM-140 surface to surface missiles. Those were the bombs that hit the cities. I'm guessing the eighth was detonated using the warhead alone, and as for the final bomb… well, it's still in the wind." He pointed at the first field in each entry. "These are the names of the ships used to deliver the missiles, followed by the explosive yield of each device, followed by the target."

Jack frowned, scanning down the list. "Hang on a second. What about the bomb that hit Seattle?"

"Seattle?" MacAuliffe shook his head. "What are you talking about? Seattle didn't get hit."

Jack's mouth fell slack as he stared at the colonel. "Are you serious?"

"Of course I'm serious. They didn't have any ships that far north, and the missiles didn't have nearly enough range to reach Seattle."

"Jesus. All this time I…" Jack's voice trailed off. He couldn't believe it. All this time he thought he'd had a narrow escape from the city. He'd thought he was only alive because Warren had taken pity on him and flown him out moments before the city had been obliterated, and now… now he knew he'd have been just fine if he'd stayed in the city. He'd spent the last day and a half running toward nuclear explosions, and away from a city that stood intact. Hell, he could have returned to the restaurant, collected the briefcase he'd left beneath the table and finished his bottle of wine.

He brushed the thought aside. It wouldn't have mattered at the end of the day. Of *course* he couldn't have done that. Even if he'd known Seattle would be perfectly safe he knew he couldn't have stayed, not while Karen and Emily were in danger. Maybe somewhere in the endless multiverse there was a version of Jack Archer who would have stayed behind and cowered in safety, but if Jack ever met that version of himself he'd gladly kick his ass. His path had been set from the moment he picked up the phone and heard Cesar Ramos on the end of the line. As soon as he'd heard that Karen was hurt.

He turned back to the page. "Now this one I recognize," he said, pointing to the Portland entry. "I was in the air when it went off."

"Portland?" MacAuliffe nodded. "Yeah, they screwed that one up something fierce. Lucky bastards. Oregon's state flower must be the four leaf clover."

"They screwed it up? What do you mean?"

"What do you mean, what do I mean?" he asked. "They missed the damned city!"

"You mean they were actually *aiming* for Portland? Seriously? I thought it went off somewhere around Eugene. That's... what, about a hundred miles south?"

MacAuliffe nodded. "Sure, but you have to bear in mind that we're talking about a missile that travels at Mach 3. It can cover a hundred miles in about two and a half minutes, so a near miss is anything that lands in the same state."

"Still, though, that's a pretty distant near miss."

"I guess so," the colonel shrugged. "Anyway, they fouled it up. As far as we can tell it wasn't supposed to be a high altitude detonation at all. It was supposed to be a standard surface impact just like the others, but something must have gone wrong. It flew straight as an arrow toward the city until it hit the coast." MacAuliffe pulled a new cigar from his pocket, rolling it between his fingers. "I guess someone on the ship screwed up, because at the last second it turned on a dime and shot off south west toward Willamette Forest."

"That's where we were," said Jack. "We'd just flown over Willamette when we saw the blast. Damn thing knocked out our engine."

MacAuliffe nodded. "Yeah? Well, I guess your loss was Portland's gain. Christ knows why, but when they gave up on hitting the target they took it up to forty thousand feet, dialed it in for maximum yield and tried to knock out every circuit on the west coast. Almost worked, too. If the missile had the fuel to reach eighty thousand feet the boys at Beale tell me they might have triggered an EMP hundreds of miles across. Lucky for us they only managed to trigger a local event."

Jack shivered at the thought. It had taken him hours to reach the edge of the blackout zone, and the effort had damn near killed him. The idea of the entire coast being plunged into darkness, every car immobilized, every light blown... it didn't bear thinking about.

"It was a lucky escape for Portland, too," MacAuliffe continued. "Seems there was a pileup on highway 84 that had everything jammed up all the way back from Troutdale. There were still maybe two hundred thousand people stuck in the city when the missile was launched, and if it had hit its target..." MacAuliffe trailed off, chewing thoughtfully on the end of his cigar.

"I can't help but wonder if God stepped in to lend a hand," he eventually continued. "See, every other city on the coast evacuated pretty smoothly. I mean, as well as you could hope for under the circumstances. Most people managed to get out before the attacks, but Portland... Portland was a God damn nightmare. Everything that could go wrong did go wrong. The main routes out of the city have been jammed up by roadworks for weeks, so it didn't take long for everything to fall to pieces. As soon as the missile was launched the military channels were flooded with reports that it was gonna be a bloodbath, and then just like that," he snapped his fingers. "Just like that it veers off course. How else do you explain that but divine intervention?"

Jack thought about it for a moment. "Well, either that or... no, never mind." He waved away a half formed thought and pointed at the words scrawled in red by the list. *Why dial them down?* "What's this?"

MacAuliffe frowned, plucking the paper from Jack's hand. "This," he sighed, "is the thing that's been pecking at my brain all day. This is the thing that doesn't make a lick of God damned sense." He stabbed a finger at the Portland entry. "The W80 warhead is what we call variable yield, or dial-a-yield to the folks in the business of blowing shit up. I don't pretend to understand how it works – something to do with tritium gas injection or some such sorcery – but the long and short of it is that the operator can remotely adjust the explosive power of the warhead right up until a few seconds before detonation."

He tapped the entry for the *MC Nakharov*. "See this here? The folks at the Pentagon estimate that the W80 out on the *Nakharov* exploded with a yield of something like twenty five kilotons. It's seems safe to say these guys weren't planning to detonate that bomb on the boat. I figure they were planning to hit San Diego, but when we sent out a bunch of Marines to board the ship they got spooked and blew it early. Now I'd bet my left butt cheek that twenty five kilotons was the default yield set up for the device. I'm guessing they didn't have time to set a custom yield before they had to blow the thing."

He pointed back to the Portland entry. "Now the W80 they detonated over Oregon was dialed all the way up to 150 kilotons. That's the maximum possible yield for this warhead. They set it at one fifty because they wanted to create an EMP, and for that you want as powerful an explosion as possible. But look at the rest of the attacks."

He ran a finger down the list. "All the other bombs, all five of them, were dialed down to just five kilotons. That's the lowest possible yield, only a third as powerful as the bomb we dropped on Hiroshima." MacAuliffe shook his head, staring down at the list with a frown. "That's… in nuclear terms that's a cherry bomb. It's a firecracker, a damned warning shot across the bows. It doesn't make any sense."

Jack suspected he was missing something, some

obvious detail that would make everything clear. He could sense something hovering right at the edge of his mind, but when he reached out to grasp it it slipped away.

"You're right," he muttered. "There's just something... I don't know, something *off* about the whole thing."

"You can say that again." MacAuliffe pulled the cigar from his mouth and tossed it on the dash. "If you have access to nukes and you're crazy enough to use them, why would you dial the yield down to the lowest possible power? They obviously knew how to do it, so whoever fired those nukes made a *choice* to dial them down. *Why?*"

Jack felt a chill pass through him. "Wait. You're not suggesting they didn't want to do much damage because they're planning to invade, are you?"

MacAuliffe shook his head. "No, I don't think so. It wouldn't make any sense. If they planned to invade their first priority would be to take out C2."

"C2?"

"Command and control," MacAuliffe explained. "They'd want to target the command structure from the President on down. If you can knock out links in the chain of command you can throw a nation into disarray and soften it up for invasion, so by the time you get boots on the ground everyone's running around like headless chickens. If invasion was the objective the first target would almost certainly have been Washington D.C., then key military sites."

He held up the list. "This, though... this just doesn't make any sense. If you're a nation state looking to invade you take out C2, then before anyone knows what hit 'em you roll in the tanks with Motörhead playing on the loudspeakers like a God damn baddass. If you're a terrorist group with limited resources you go for whichever target gives you the biggest bang for your buck, and the toughest psychological blow. You fly a jet into the Twin Towers or set off a dirty bomb on the National Mall. You blow up Times Square and make sure every camera on the planet is pointed at it, then you claim responsibility, sit back and enjoy the chaos. But this?" He shook his head. "Nuking Fresno? Bakersfield? These targets have no strategic value. They don't even have much *cultural* value."

"Well," Jack protested mildly, "to be fair they were pretty nice cities."

"Huh? No, that's not what I mean," MacAuliffe replied. "I'm sure they were just fine, but these cities don't exist in the... I guess you'd call it the national psyche. They don't hold a place in our hearts, not like New York or LA. Most people have never been to either of them, and they don't have a mental picture in their head. Destroying them when you've already taken out LA and San Francisco is just... well, it's a hat on a hat, know what I mean? In strategic terms it's a waste of a good nuke. It's overkill, but at the same time it's *underkill*."

"How do you mean?"

"I mean doing all this, needlessly attacking all of these cities, but then dialing the warheads back to five kilotons. It just doesn't make strategic sense. It hardly makes any difference on the ground. A five kiloton nuke will flatten every last building in a half mile radius from the blast, and a hundred fifty kiloton bomb will do the same over a mile and a half. The city's destroyed either way, so why not go for maximum damage? Why would you half ass a nuclear attack?"

Jack pondered the question, still feeling as if there was something obvious waiting just beyond his view. "Well... is that the *only* difference? Between five and one fifty kilotons, I mean. Is it just a slightly bigger blast radius?"

MacAuliffe shrugged. "Pretty much, yeah." He fell silent for a moment. "I guess the mushroom cloud on the one fifty would be a lot bigger, but apart from that... yeah, there's not a whole lot of difference."

"How much bigger? In terms of altitude, I mean."

The colonel frowned, leafing through his bundle of papers. "Hold on, I've got the projections here somewhere." Eventually he picked the right sheet from the bundle. "OK, here we go. Ummm... OK, yeah. The cloud from a five kiloton blast would top out at around fifteen thousand feet. A one fifty blast would be... somewhere around forty four thousand. Why?"

"Hmmm." Jack sat back, scratching his stubble as he thought. The seed of an idea was forming in his head. He wasn't quite sure if it made any sense, but he wanted to hear it out loud. Maybe the colonel could poke enough holes to sink it, but maybe... maybe it made sense.

"OK, bear with me, I'm just throwing everything at the wall and seeing what sticks." He spoke slowly, deliberately. "So imagine you're a bad guy. Foreign government, Bin Laden's even more evil twin brother, doesn't matter. You're a bad guy, you've decided you're mad at the States and you have a bunch of nukes burning a hole in your pocket."

MacAuliffe nodded. "OK, I'll bite. I'm a bad guy. What am I doing now?"

"You've already detonated one warhead way out in the ocean where it barely kills anyone, but now you've been discovered. We've noticed your other ships, and we know you can launch against us at any moment." Jack paused for a moment, still working out his theory as he spoke.

"But you *don't*. You could have caught us with our pants down. You could have killed millions before we'd even figured out what you're doing, but instead you wait, what, two, three hours before launching the rest of your missiles?"

MacAuliffe chewed on his cigar for a moment before speaking. "Maybe you caught *me* with my pants down. Maybe I'm not ready yet. Maybe I have to plot in the guidance or coordinate the attacks with the other ships."

"Maybe," Jack conceded, "but for whatever reason you hold off while the cities start to evacuate. You're losing victims by the minute. And then you launch all six of your missiles at the same time. All six are headed for cities, but a few minutes before they reach their targets you hear that one of them hasn't evacuated yet. There are still hundreds of thousands of people stuck there, and rather than kill them all you decide to send your missile off course."

"So you think they didn't want to kill people?"

Jack shook his head. "No, of course they did. If they didn't want to kill people they would have gone to the movies instead of nuking six cities. I'm just saying maybe they didn't want to kill *millions* of people. I'm saying maybe it was the *spectacle* they were looking for, not the body count. They wanted the imagery of an entire coast destroyed, cities large and small razed to the ground, but they wanted to do it with as few deaths as they could get away with."

MacAuliffe shook his head, confused.

"But if they're trying to kill as few people as possible, why allow people to evacuate the cities and then attack them again when they reach the refugee camp?"

Jack frowned. "Now *that* I can't answer." He thought about it for a moment before something struck him. "But then again… I mean, they didn't *actually* blow up the camp, did they?"

"They damn well tried. If our guys hadn't found that truck we'd be looking at tens of thousands dead."

"Maybe, but maybe not." Jack turned it over in his

head. "How do you detonate a bomb like the W80? It's designed to be mounted on a missile, right? Not just set off on its own?"

The colonel nodded. "That's right. The W80 is essentially just a modified B61 gravity bomb. The original design was intended to be dropped from a bomber, and the basic setup of the W80 wasn't much changed when it was modified for use as a warhead. *Usually* the detonation would be triggered on impact with the ground, but obviously that wasn't the case here. I can only imagine it was triggered in laydown mode."

"Laydown mode?"

"Yeah, it's a… a delayed detonation. There's a time delay fuse that holds the detonation long enough for the bomber to clear the area. It's designed for low altitude drops, because a pilot would never clear the blast radius in time if he released for a ground burst at a couple hundred feet. Laydown mode isn't really useful for the W80 since it's missile mounted, but they didn't bother to change the design between models."

"OK, so someone… what, lit the fuse and ran?"

"No, son," MacAuliffe shook his head, chuckling at Jack's understanding of nuclear weapons. "The warhead doesn't have Acme written on the side in big letters. This isn't a fuse like you'd get in a firework. It's electronic. And besides, you couldn't just set it and run. The fuse on a W80 isn't like an egg timer. It's set for exactly 31 seconds, and it's completely tamperproof. You can't adjust the timing, and you can't replace it without disabling the device. You trigger the bomb remotely, and then 31 seconds later it…"

MacAuliffe trailed off for a moment. He'd finally figured out what Jack was saying. "My God, *they* decided when to detonate the bomb. Without the satellite network they must have been close enough to trigger it by line of sight. That means they were no more than a few dozen miles away when it went off. They were *watching*."

"They never *planned* to blow up the safe zone," Jack nodded. "They *wanted* your men to find it, and they waited until your captain got it far enough away from the camp before they set it off. Maybe the message they were trying to send is *We're not done yet. We can still hurt you no matter how far you run.*" He shrugged. "Or maybe they're just insane. What do I know?"

For a moment MacAuliffe sat in silence, staring

out the window deep in thought. "OK," he finally said. "Let's say you're right about all of this. Let's say I agree that they didn't plan to kill millions of people, and they're just trying to… what, just terrorize us? All of that I can buy, but I still don't get one thing." He turned back to Jack. "What does any of this have to do with the size of the mushroom clouds?"

Jack pointed up at the sky. "The jet stream."

MacAuliffe frowned. "What about it?"

"High altitude winds start at around twenty thousand feet, blowing a gale west to east at more than a hundred miles per hour. If you detonate a five kiloton bomb at ground level the mushroom cloud will top out at… what did you say, fifteen thousand? I'm only guessing, but I'd imagine the worst of the fallout would drift just a few dozen miles before it reaches the ground. Maybe a hundred at a pinch. People in the immediate area would be pretty screwed, but in the grand scheme of things it's not the end of the world."

MacAuliffe glanced in the rear view mirror at the mushroom cloud that was already collapsing, drifting back to the ground. "But if you get the fallout high enough to enter the jet stream…"

"You get babies in Ohio born with gills." Jack gave

MacAuliffe a weak smile. "Think about it. The only bomb they dialed up to a hundred fifty kilotons was the one they detonated in the atmosphere, where it wouldn't generate any appreciable fallout. All the other missiles were dialed back just enough to keep the damage from spreading beyond the west coast. It's as if whoever did this went out of their way to do something as destructive as possible, but with as few fatalities as possible."

MacAuliffe shook his head in disbelief. "I just... OK, I can see how that makes some kind of sense, but the question remains: *why?* Why would an enemy attack us like this if they want to minimize casualties? Why launch a nuclear attack if you don't want to kill millions of people?"

Jack threw up his hands. "I can't even begin to imagine." He shrugged and puffed out his cheeks, "I have no idea how to even get into the mindset of someone crazy enough to launch a nuke, let alone a bunch of them." He leaned back in his seat and chewed on his thumbnail. "I mean... well, the only way it makes any sense to me is if we staged the attacks ourselves and wanted to make it look *insanely* convincing. But that'd be crazy, of course."

MacAuliffe turned slowly in his seat to face Jack,

his eyes wide and his face suddenly drained of color. Jack met his gaze, confused.

"Why are you looking at me like that?"

●▼●

CHAPTER ELEVEN
JUST LIKE MY FATHER

"I DON'T THINK it's broken."

Karen perched on the rattling tailgate of the tan brown troop truck, clinging to the frame to keep herself from being jolted out when the tires hit one of the countless potholes in the road. With her free hand she held Emily tight around the waist as she watched Ramos tending to Krasinski's wrist. His surgery was a few square feet of clear space in amongst the dozens of wooden crates that loomed over their heads.

"It *feels* broken," Ted winced, resting the tender, swollen arm in his free hand. "Can you check again? I can barely move my hand."

Ramos shook his head, grabbing a bottle of

Tylenol from one of the open crates. "Just a good sprain, Ted," he assured him, popping the cap from the bottle and shaking out a few tablets. "I'm pretty sure you'll live. And hey, look on the bright side. After years in accounting you've finally got a good story to impress girls. You survived a helicopter crash and jumped from the wreckage in the shadow of a mushroom cloud." He grinned and patted him on the shoulder. "That's gotta be worth at least first base, right?"

Ted grimaced. "Well thanks, but you managed to get the same story, and *you* got through it without a scratch."

"I guess some of us have all the luck," Ramos shrugged. "All I can say is suck it up." He lowered his voice, nodding his head in Valerie's direction. "And count yourself lucky you got out with just a sprained wrist, huh? Could have been a hell of a lot worse."

Ted turned to find Valerie sitting alone on top of a crate in the depths of the truck, her knees tucked up to her chest. He nodded in agreement and lowered his voice to match Ramos'. "Yeah, OK, I get you."

Valerie had barely spoken a word since the crash. She'd withdrawn into herself the moment the adrenaline had burned itself out. When the heart thumping fight or flight energy abandoned her she'd been left with nothing but the terrible realization that the pilot had sacrificed his life to save her. Karen watched as Ramos carefully approached and hopped up beside her on the crate, and she wasn't at all surprised to see Valerie turn away from him as he tried to comfort her.

Karen understood how she was feeling. She wasn't ready to deal with people yet. She wasn't ready for the comforting hug, and and she definitely wasn't ready for the schmaltzy *it's not your fault* Good Will Hunting pep talk. Before she could get there she needed to brood a little first. She needed to sit alone in the dark with her thoughts. She needed to let the guilt take her to pieces before she could begin to put herself back together, and Karen knew that right now one train of thought in particular would be much, *much* louder than all the others.

Why me? Why did I survive and he died? What makes me so special?

Karen was all too familiar with those questions. They'd been running through her head on a loop ever since Ramos had found her in the hospital back in the city. Ever since they'd left the building, knowing they were leaving hundreds of other patients behind to die. She knew the Doc had only come to find her because he'd made a promise to Jack, but the hospital was *full* of people just as deserving of life, and nobody had come to save *them*.

She'd asked herself again as they passed evacuees running towards the bridge. Maybe not so much with the looters – they'd made their own bed – but the people running to escape the city while Karen shot by in the Corvette? Surely *they* hadn't deserved to die.

Again when the bridge collapsed, when she'd looked down at the lower deck and locked eyes with a man trapped beneath a concrete block. When the upper level collapsed down on him and the people trying to save him Karen couldn't help but wonder why she was allowed to escape, but the Samaritans who'd risked their lives to help weren't offered the same gift, and all because she'd chosen one deck and they'd taken the other.

Finally she'd asked herself when she saw the woman in the pharmacy crouched over her dying husband, not understanding that he wasn't going to make it. What had they done to deserve such a terrible fate? Why had the world decreed that this poor woman should spend her final hours watching her husband die in agony? What crime could she possibly have committed to earn that sentence?

The whole thing was just flat out ass backwards. There was no rhyme or reason. People died on the flip of a coin, good or bad, right or wrong, and the Pats kept winning the Super Bowl no matter how often everyone else thanked Jesus for their touchdowns. After two days and two nukes Karen was still breathing, and there wasn't a damn thing she could think of to explain why she'd been allowed to sail through it all as if she were invincible.

Was it really just dumb luck? Was it really as simple as choosing to turn left instead of right, rolling the dice and hoping for the best, or was there some divine hand guiding her, making sure she wove the perfect path through a world that was falling to pieces around her? Was there some force leading the way, helping her miraculously escape the disasters that killed those judged less deserving?

She pulled Emily a little closer and sighed. Honestly, she didn't know what terrified her more. She didn't know whether she'd prefer to live in a chaotic, uncaring, Godless world, as random and cruel as the roll of a die, or a world in which God had decided to help her out and screw everyone else.

And now... now Valerie would be asking herself

those same questions, but in her case it would be a thousand times worse. She'd have to go through the rest of her life wondering not only why she was spared while other died, but whether she was truly worthy of the life the pilot had traded for his own. She'd have to spend the rest of her life wondering if fate had struck a fair bargain. Whether the world was better with her in it, or if the pilot had sacrificed himself for nothing.

"Penny for your thoughts?"

Karen's attention snapped back to the present, and she realized she'd been staring back at the mushroom cloud with glazed eyes, not really seeing it. Krasinski crouched beside her, his torn corduroy jacket flapping gently in the breeze that crept through the open tailgate.

"Sorry, Ted," she replied, flustered. "I was a million miles away. I was just thinking... oh, never mind. I don't suppose it matters."

Krasinski awkwardly lowered himself down to the tailgate, steadying himself with his one good hand. For a moment he wobbled, almost toppling out the back before he found his balance, and Karen breathed a sigh of relief when he finally took his seat.

"What's with this stuff?" He pointed at her left

arm, her hand clinging to the steel ribbing that supported the canvas roof. A needle ran from just below the inside of her elbow, and from it a thin length of tubing ran back to an IV bag that hung from the frame of the truck. "You OK?"

Karen nodded. She'd almost forgotten it was there. "Oh, yeah. It's nothing. I think it's called Filgrastim. It's, umm, a treatment for radiation sickness. The Doc found it in one of the crates."

"Wow, seriously? You have radiation sickness?" Krasinski seemed almost impressed.

Karen chuckled. "I doubt I'm the only one, Ted. Maybe you noticed the enormous mushroom cloud about ten miles behind us?"

Krasinski gave her a bashful smile. "Yeah, I suppose you're right. I guess it's about as common as the flu right now. Are you gonna be OK?"

"Yeah, I think I'll live," Karen replied, with more confidence than she felt. "Doc said it's just a precaution. Something to do with boosting my white count. Though if I make it through this I think I'm gonna be sporting the punk look for a while." She reached up and ran her fingers through her hair, and her hand came away with a dozen loose strands. "I don't think there's anything back here that'll save my hair."

Krasinski grinned and rubbed his hand across his bald head. "If you find something, I've got dibs. Seriously, though, shouldn't you be in hospital right now? If you'd told me you had radiation sickness we never would have sent you to the safe zone. We have doctors back at the base."

Karen tapped the IV bag. "This is the reason we were headed to the safe zone. We didn't know where else we could find this stuff."

"But you're sure you're OK? I mean, we could always– "

"Honestly, Ted, I'm fine," Karen interrupted. "I'm trying not to think about it. Sorry. Can we maybe change the subject?"

"Sure, sure," Ted nodded. "No problem at all." He fell silent for a while, looking back at the gray cloud of ash and dust billowing thousands of feet above them in the distance. Eventually he let out a long sigh. "I wonder how many people died back there."

Karen shot him a sidelong glance. "I was really hoping we could change the subject a little further than that, Ted. Maybe we can shoot for something that doesn't involve talking about death?"

"Sorry." Krasinski blushed, awkwardly adjusting

his torn jacket. "I'm afraid I was never all that good at small talk. Years locked in a small room slaving over a calculator. The job doesn't encourage the development of a sparkling wit, know what I mean?"

Karen snorted. "If you think that's bad you should try being a parent. Endless hours of Peppa Pig and Dora the Explorer turn your brain to mush after a while. Kids' TV should come with a health warning for parents. Either that or free wine." She squeezed Emily a little tighter and looked up at Krasinski. "Do you have any kids?"

"Me?" He crinkled his nose with mock distaste and shook his head. "No, I never pulled that trigger. My ex-wife wanted a whole posse of rugrats, but honestly I couldn't imagine anything worse."

"You can't imagine anything worse than kids?" She nodded toward the mushroom cloud. "You know a nuke went off right over there about a half hour ago, right?"

Krasinski laughed. "You know what I mean. I like things neat and tidy. Everything in its proper place. I just can't imagine anything worse than sharing a home with a little monster who exists to make a mess. Kids are… well, they're sticky."

"*Sticky?*"

"Yeah. I don't know what it is about them, but they seem to walk around all day using jars of peanut butter and jelly as mittens." He narrowed his eyes. "You never noticed that? Half the stuff they touch gets covered in a layer of their last meal, and the other half ends up dripping with snot."

Emily frowned up at Krasinski. "*I'm* not sticky. I'm not sticky, right mom?"

Karen shook her head. "Of course you're not, pumpkin," Karen assured her. "You're perfect." She pulled Emily towards her and planted a kiss on the top of her head, and while she wasn't looking Karen looked up at Krasinski and nodded with a sly smile.

"So," she said, changing the subject as Emily shot daggers from her eyes, "what do you think this is all about?"

Krasinski shifted awkwardly on the tailgate, trying to ignore Emily's judgmental glare. "All what about?"

"This." Karen gestured towards the mushroom cloud. "All of it. Why do you think our own people would want to launch nukes at us?"

Krasinski sniffed, scratching his bald dome as he gazed back at the destruction. "Well," he said, squinting against the bright sunlight. "You'd have to ask an expert, but I've been working with the military for more than two decades, and if there's one thing I've learned in all those years it's that this kind of thing always comes down to money."

"Money? How do you mean?"

"I mean exactly that. If you're looking for the motivation behind pretty much anything, go deep enough and you'll eventually find someone who thinks it'll make him a few dollars." He sniffed. "Hell, even Islamic terrorism is all about the Benjamins. Maybe not for the deluded morons who blow themselves up because they've been told they'll get a whole mess of virgins in Heaven, but go up the ladder and *abracadabra*, there's some guy sitting at the top who cares more about the paint job on his new Rolls Royce Phantom than he ever did about the Koran. It all comes down to money in the end."

Karen looked doubtful. "You really believe there are people out there willing to nuke their own country for the sake of money?"

"Karen," Krasinski sighed. "I believe there are people out there who'd be willing to nuke their own *kids* if there were enough zeroes on the check."

"Oh, come on. You can't seriously be that cynical."

"Maybe I'm cynical," he shrugged, "or maybe I've just seen so much greed that it's hard to see anything else any more. Just look at the wars we wage."

"You think *our* wars are just about money?" Karen narrowed her eyes. "I bet there are a few guys back at your base who might have an issue with you saying that."

Krasinski dismissively waved a hand. "No, think about it. When was the last truly *just* war? Y'know, the last war where we stepped in because it would have been morally offensive for us to sit back and watch from the sidelines?"

He let the question hang in the air for a few moments. "It was World War Two, right? That was the last time you could say, hand on heart, that if we'd stayed home the world would have gone to hell. That was the last time you could say that every American life lost was really worth the price, because every last soldier died trying to beat back evil."

He sighed, as if nostalgic for a simpler time. "That kind of Captain America good versus evil world only exists in the Marvel Universe now. These days we don't fight to save our civilization. We fight to protect our *interests*." He held up his hands. "And hey, don't get me wrong, I'm not saying that's a terrible thing. I'm not naïve. I know there's a damn good reason my gas doesn't cost ten dollars a gallon. We've done pretty well out of the global status quo, and sometimes you have to bring out the big guns when someone gets it in their head to screw things up for the rest of us."

Karen chuckled. "You sound just like my father."

"Oh yeah? What, is he a cynical sonofabitch too?"

"He was, yeah. He was a major in the Army. Saw a lot of action in the Gulf. If he was here right now I'm sure he'd be nodding along as you spoke, and my mom would be cheering beside him."

Krasinski laughed. "Sounds like a smart lady."

"Nah," Karen shook her head with a grin. "I mean yeah, she is, but that's not why she'd be cheering. She'd be cheering because you proved her theory."

Krasinski tilted his head. "What theory's that?"

"Just a theory she had about why my dad was so screwed up. See, ever since he came back from Iraq he was always... well, let's just say quick to anger. He was always suspicious of people who looked like they enjoyed power. He *hated* them. And I'm not just talking about obvious assholes, like guys who raise a hand to their wives. He hated, like, assistant managers at McDonalds who gave orders to the staff without a please and thank you. He hated pretty much anyone who stood above someone else and looked like they enjoyed the view. It just set him off. Made him want to start throwing punches." She looked at Emily, and noticed that the rumbling of the truck had sent her to sleep. She lowered her voice and shifted her arm around her.

"He was never like that before. Before he went to the Gulf dad was… he was Mister Rogers on steroids. He was a peacemaker. Mom always said that's why he joined the Army, to end the fight as quickly as possible." Her smile faded at the memory. "But then he spent some time at a refugee camp. Too much time, I guess. When he came home he told me all the stories. Horrible stuff. Just the worst of humanity, all the greed and cruelty and selfishness. He said he watched people in that camp fight to control it. He watched people kill each other just to be the top dog in a crappy patch of dirt out in the desert, and when he got home…" Karen sighed. "Well, that was all he could see any more. He stopped seeing the good in people. He just saw… predators, I guess. He figured the guy at McDonalds who got delusions of grandeur when he got an extra star on his badge was the same kinda guy who'd start killing people in a refugee camp if the circumstances were a little different."

"Sounds like he had a rough time out there."

"Yeah, he did," Karen nodded. "Anyway, my point is that if you asked *him* what all of this was about he'd say *power* without a moment's hesitation. He wouldn't even pause for breath. He'd think it was some wannabe Hitler who wanted to rule over the rest of us, because that was his experience." She pointed to Krasinski. "Now *you*, you've spent a lifetime working with numbers. You've spent your whole career staring at the balance sheets of war. Of *course* you think it's all about money, because that's *your* experience."

"Well, maybe," Krasinski shrugged noncommittally. "I guess we all view the world through our own personal lens, but I still think I'm right. If we ever find out why any of this happened I'd bet my ass it wasn't ideological. This thing was too well organized to be a bunch of nuts trying to bring about the end of days. Someone stands to gain from all this, and I'm betting that it all comes down to dollar signs." He fell silent for a moment, picking at a loose thread on his jacket sleeve. "What about you, though? Is there some weird psychological trauma in your past that leads you to think this is all about… I don't know, racism or blueberry donuts or something?"

Karen laughed. "I'm sure there is, Ted, but I don't like to psychoanalyze myself." Emily shifted in her sleep beside her, and she squeezed a little tighter. "No, I don't have any theories. The way I see it, the only people who could really understand why anyone would do something like this are the ones crazy enough to launch the missiles. I don't even like to kill bugs."

Karen turned at a noise behind her, and she found Ramos edging his way toward the tailgate around the stacked crates. By the look on his face he'd had no success brightened Valerie's mood, but at least she was standing up now. Behind Ramos Karen could see her on her feet beside the crates.

'Hey, Doc." She lowered her voice and nodded toward Valerie. "How's she holding up?"

"She... umm, I think she needs a little more time," he replied, stepping behind Karen and reaching for the IV bag that hung above her. "She's taking it pretty hard. How are you feeling? Any better?"

"Well, I don't feel like I'll die anytime soon, if that's what you mean." She held her arm steady as Ramos tore away a strip of tape and slid the needle from beneath her skin.

"Yeah? Give it a few hours," Ramos smiled, patting

her on the shoulder. "The side effects can be pretty rough. Lemme know if you feel any deep muscle or bone aches coming on. I can give– " He reached out to steady himself against the frame of the truck as it suddenly slowed, and he almost lost his footing as they took a sharp left turn. "Whoa, nearly went down there. That would have been embarrassing. What was I saying?"

Karen pressed her hand against the puncture wound on her forearm. "I think you were displaying a little more of that world beating bedside manner, Doc. Something about terrible side effects and bone aches?"

"Oh, yeah." He gave her a dismissive wave of the hand. "Don't worry, you'll probably get away with just a minor headache, but give me a yell if you feel anything worse. I can give you some painkillers to take the edge off if it gets too…" His voice trailed off. "Hey, why are we off the highway? Ted? Aren't we supposed to be headed back to Beale?"

"Hey, guys?" Karen caught Valerie's faint call from the other end of the crates, but she kept her focus on Ted.

"Yeah," Krasinski nodded, frowning. Out the back they could see the convoy continue on west back toward the base, but their truck was now alone on a narrow, dusty side road heading south. "As far as I know all the trucks were ordered back to the base."

Karen leaned her head out the back of the truck, peering around the side to see if there were any other vehicles on the road ahead. "Did you ask the driver where we were going before we climbed in? There's nobody else ahead of us."

"I..." Krasinski fumbled for words. "Well, no. I don't think the driver even knows we're on the truck, but the entire convoy was ordered back to the base. If everyone was going off in different directions it wouldn't be a convoy. It'd just be traffic."

Karen slid back from the edge of the tailgate as the truck began to bounce on the rough surface. By the look of the pockmarked, piecemeal asphalt this road hadn't been repaired in decades. "Do you know what's in this direction? I don't suppose this could be a shortcut to the base?" she asked, optimistically.

"Shortcut?" Krasinski shook his head. "Not a chance. The highway runs in pretty much a straight line all the way back to Beale. This is... I don't know, due south? There's just a whole lot of nothing in this direction. Well, nothing apart from an old airfield, but it's been abandoned for years."

"Hey! Guys!" Now Valerie was more insistent, her voice louder. Ramos turned back to her.

"You OK?" he asked. "What do you need?"

"I'm fine," Valerie insisted, a sharp edge in her voice, "but I think we may have a problem here."

Karen pulled herself up from the tailgate, lifting Emily in her arms, and she followed Ramos back into the depths of the truck. "What is it?"

"I was sitting on this crate, and I broke through the lid." She raised a warning finger at Ramos. "If you make a joke about my ass I swear to God I'll throw you out the back, Cesar Ramos."

Ramos paused, his mouth open, and then thought better of it. "Are you hurt?"

Valerie shook her head. "No, I'm fine, but look at this." She'd pulled aside the splintered wooden slats from the top of the crate, revealing a glimpse of its contents. "This ain't good, right?"

Karen and Ramos looked down into the crate.

"Ted?" Karen turned back to the tailgate. "Can you come take a look at this?"

Krasinski hauled himself up from the floor with difficulty, and on unsteady legs he made his way into the darkness. When he reached the crate Ramos moved aside to allow him through, and he peered down at the gap in the crate.

"This truck's supposed to be carrying just medical supplies, right?" Ramos asked.

Krasinski's face had lost all of its color. "Can I… can I please have the pry bar?"

"Tell me this isn't what I think it is," Ramos demanded, passing Krasinski the bar they'd used to lever open the other crates.

"Just a second." His voice was wobbly and strained as he drove the bar into the gap beneath the lid, With a little effort he rocked it back and forth until the lid popped free.

"Ted, tell me!"

Krasinski stared down into the open crate, his eyes wide and his face an ashen white.

"No, doctor, it's exactly what you think it is." He let the pry bar slip from his hand, and it hit the ground with a loud clang. "This is a nuclear warhead."

•▼•

CHAPTER TWELVE
THE INCIRLIK ARSENAL

JACK LEANED FORWARD on the edge of his seat, listening intently as Colonel MacAuliffe struggled to connect with the convoy leading back to Beale from the destroyed safe zone. From the sound of the signal he guessed they were at the very limits of the radio's range.

"I'm sorry, sir," a voice crackled across the airwaves, so faint it was almost inaudible over the static hiss. "Could you please repeat your last? I'm not certain I'm reading you."

MacAuliffe swore under his breath before raising the radio once more to his lips. "I say again: I need to know the name of the person who located the warhead. Shouldn't be a difficult question, son. I just need to know who found the truck."

There was a long silence before the voice returned. "Yes sir, I understand. I'm just waiting for... hold on, please." The sound of several mumbling voices drifted from the radio before the speaker returned. "I'm told it was Staff Sergeant Danvers, sir."

"Danvers?" MacAuliffe frowned, scratching his head. "Can't say I recognize the name. He's not one of mine, is he?"

"From Beale? No sir, he's National Guard. He came in on a transport from Camp Roberts early this morning, sir."

"Now Lieutenant," MacAuliffe replied, "this is very important. Was Danvers alone when he found the bomb? What was he doing when he found it? Did he have a good reason to be there?"

"Umm... yes sir, I believe he was alone." The Lieutenant sounded confused about the line of questioning. "I... well, I couldn't tell you if he had a good reason to be there. The enlisted men from Roberts were assigned to construction duties on the far side of the camp, so I'm not sure what he was doing in the vehicle bay. All I know is that he reported the discovery to Captain Standish, and the Captain took it to General Bailey."

For a moment MacAuliffe stared out at the road ahead, tapping the antenna of the radio against his teeth, deep in thought. Finally he clicked the transmit button once more. "Lieutenant," he sighed, "I need you to take Staff Sergeant Danvers into custody immediately."

"Sir?"

"You heard me, Lieutenant. I'm ordering you to have Danvers placed under arrest. I want him isolated and under guard right away, you understand? We'll be back at Beale in…" he glanced at his watch, "about fifteen minutes. Bring him directly to me when you arrive. Is that understood?"

"Understood, sir."

"Good man. Out."

MacAuliffe dropped the radio into his lap and turned to Jack. "I damn sure hope you're wrong, Jack," he said. "It's a crying shame to have to place one of your own men under arrest, but I think you might be onto something."

"Well, hold on a second," Jack protested. "That was just… y'know, just brainstorming. I was just tossing out ideas. I didn't mean to get a sergeant arrested!"

"Better safe than sorry, Jack," MacAuliffe assured

him. "And besides, it was my call. You don't need to feel guilty about it."

Jack couldn't believe how quickly this was moving. Just a minute ago he'd been idly joking that the attacks could have been an inside job, and now... now a sergeant he'd never even met was on his way to a set of handcuffs. "This is insane, colonel. It's just crazy! Why on earth would you listen to me about this? It's not like there's any evidence to support it, is there? It's just speculation!"

MacAuliffe looked away awkwardly, his chin tucked in to his neck as he peered down at the papers in his hands.

Jack narrowed his eyes. "It *is* just speculation, right? Colonel?"

"Don't worry about it,"MacAuliffe scowled. He looked into Jack's eyes and saw nothing but questions. "There are some things that have to remain classified."

"Are there? It's like you said yourself, there's no way any of this will stay secret for long. You might as well just tell me what's going on." He waited for MacAuliffe to start talking, but the colonel remained stubbornly silent. The tension in the Humvee seemed to grow with each passing second, and just as it felt the silence might take on physical form and beat him over the head a thought occurred to Jack.

"Wait a minute," he said, waving a finger in the air. "You never answered my question."

MacAuliffe coughed and turned to look out the window, his mood clearly turning defensive. "And which question was that?"

"I asked you, back when I saw the nuke list. I asked you how you knew how many bombs were out there, and you never answered."

"Oh, for Christ's sake, Jack," MacAuliffe groaned, "you're killing me here."

Jack pressed on, undeterred. "Captain Standish said something about the serial number matching some itinerary. He said something about an arsenal, didn't he? Insilit? Interlink?"

The colonel seemed to visibly shrink before Jack's eyes. He slumped in his seat and sighed, his resolve broken. "Hell, if you can figure out this much after overhearing a single conversation I dread to think what a journalist might be able to glean." He lowered his voice, glancing over Jack's shoulder to ensure Cathy and Garside couldn't hear him.

"Alright, Jack, I'm gonna level with you, but this conversation doesn't leave this truck, understand?"

Jack nodded. "Understood."

"The word you heard was Incirlik," MacAuliffe whispered. "Standish was talking about the Incirlik arsenal."

"Incirlik?" The word meant nothing to him. "Is that an acronym for something?"

MacAuliffe shook his head. "No, son, it's not an acronym. Incirlik is the name of a Turkish air base in Adana, a city in southern Turkey." He took a deep breath and closed his eyes before speaking again. "And it's from Incirlik that nine nuclear weapons were stolen in 2016."

Jack reeled back in shock. He didn't know how to respond. For years he'd heard conspiracy theories about lost and stolen nuclear weapons, most of them delivered by foaming at the mouth nut jobs on talk radio shows, but here was an Air Force colonel confirming matter-of-factually that it had actually happened. It was *real*. There were nukes out there in the hands of God knew who, just waiting to be dropped on an unsuspecting country.

"Stolen? Are you serious?" He shook his head, struggling to believe it could be true, and then a question occurred to him. "Wait, did you say a *Turkish* air base? Since when was Turkey a nuclear power?"

MacAuliffe chewed at his lower lip, clearly unhappy to be divulging these secrets, but eventually he continued. "You don't understand, Jack," he said, lowering his voice until it was little higher than a whisper. "I'm not talking about Turkish weapons. Incirlik Air Base is controlled by the Turkish Air Force, but it's a joint base. We've been using it as a hub for air missions over Russia and the Middle East ever since the Cold War."

"No." Jack couldn't bring himself to believe it. "Don't tell me these weapons are American."

MacAuliffe nodded solemnly. "I'm afraid they are."

"You're seriously telling me that the US had nine nukes just sitting at an air base in Turkey? You're telling me that somebody stole them and nobody ever found out about it?"

"That's what I'm telling you," MacAuliffe confirmed. "In fact, I'm telling you that we had *fifty* nukes sitting at Incirlik, but only nine were stolen. They've been there for years, and as far as anyone outside the US knows all fifty are still safely tucked in their bunker to this day."

"Nobody knows? You didn't even tell the Turkish government?"

MacAuliffe let out an incredulous laugh. "Of course not. When you have an empty quiver incident you don't just blurt it out to– "

"I'm sorry," Jack interrupted. "Empty quiver?"

"Yeah, it's the term we use for an incident involving the theft of a functioning nuclear weapon."

"Jesus," Jack whispered. "It's scary that we even *have* a term for that."

"Well, anyway, you don't go public when you lose a nuke. You don't say *anything* until you absolutely have to. Can you imagine what kind of world we'd be living in if people knew there were loose nukes just floating around? Hell, the panic alone could be enough to push us all to the brink of nuclear war. It'd be the Cuban Missile Crisis all over again, with every nuclear state just hovering over the button, waiting for someone to blink. So no, we didn't tell the Turkish government. We decided to deal with it in house."

Jack nodded back towards the remains of the mushroom cloud. "Well it looks like you guys didn't do a great job of it."

MacAuliffe glared at Jack. "Hey, don't look at me. The Incirlik theft triggered one of the largest covert investigations in US history, but I wasn't involved. I spent 2016 sitting in a baking hot office in Bagram directing drone missions."

"So who *was* in charge?"

MacAuliffe shrugged. "Every agency with an acronym had skin in the game. CIA, NSA, DIA, INSCOM… they brought in everyone who could be trusted to get the job done and keep their mouth shut, but a year later they had the square root of jack shit to show for it. Whoever stole those weapons were *ghosts*. No obvious motive, no clear affiliation. Not even any whispers along the usual terrorist networks. That's… that's *impossible*. Outside of a James Bond movie you just don't get to be a super villain without someone knowing about it. You can't pull off a heist like this without someone somewhere letting something slip. You can't even *recruit* for a job this big without the intelligence agencies picking up at least a hint that something's going down."

"Why not? Terrorists can't keep secrets?"

"It's not about keeping secrets. Something on this scale leaves its mark. It has… it's hard to explain, but something like this has its own *gravity*. It distorts everything around it in a way that any seasoned agent should be able to recognize. High profile figures vanish and leave a vacuum. Low level henchmen show up where they're not supposed to be. Money gets moved from place to place. A nuclear heist should have left a breadcrumb trail right across the world, but there was *nothing*."

"So they never figured out who did it?"

MacAuliffe shook his head. "They didn't even have a working theory. However these guys operated it was entirely outside of the known terror and criminal networks, and it damned sure wasn't state sponsored. It was almost as if a random bunch of people with clean records and no prior connections just got together over coffee one morning and decided to lift a bunch of nukes. It was just *baffling*."

MacAuliffe leaned back in his seat and sighed. "Anyway, we spent the last three years waiting for the other shoe to drop. We knew the nukes would eventually pop up on the radar somewhere on the planet. I just never expected it would be here."

Jack stared at the colonel, waiting for him to break into a grin and tell him he was just pulling his leg, but there wasn't a trace of humor in his expression. "What… when… how could…" he trailed off, taking a moment to gather his thoughts. "Even if you don't know who did this, how is it possible for anyone to steal a bunch of nuclear weapons from a military base? Aren't these things stored deep underground and surrounded by about a million armed guards? You can't just walk in and grab them off the shelf, right?"

"Of course not. It's easier to get into the damned Oval Office than it is to get within a hundred yards of a nuke. There's nothing in the world more closely guarded. You'd almost need to use a nuke against a base just to cause enough panic and confusion to get close enough to the nukes." He let out a dry, humorless chuckle. "Or, if you decided that brute force wasn't the answer, you could just wait for a coup to destabilize the country surrounding the base, and then piggyback on the chaos. You remember the 2016 Turkish coup, right?"

Once again Jack searched for signs of humor, and once again he came up wanting. "No… you can't be serious. You're telling me that they just sat around waiting for a coup to magically happen, and then took the opportunity to swoop in?"

"Not exactly, no. Look, I don't know what you know about the inner workings of Turkey, but this wasn't just luck. The coup was always going to happen sooner or later. There were so many people who despised President Erdogan – including many at the highest levels of the Turkish military – that it was only a matter of time before someone decided to try to bring down his government. What's more, the commander of Incirlik Air Base was a man named Brigadier General Bekir Ercan Van. His hostility to the President were well known, and when the coup finally began it was no surprise that the general came down on the side of the putschists."

"What happened?"

"What happened was he allowed the putschists to use the base to launch bombing missions on government buildings. He was arrested for it, of course. In fact later he applied for political asylum here in the US, but what matters is what happened the night of the coup."

Jack sat on the edge of his seat, enthralled. "Yeah?"

"The folks who lifted the nukes knew the Turkish playbook. They knew that the first thing the government would do is cut power to the base. We begged them for years to stop using this dumbass strategy, and we were begging specifically because it made it more difficult to protect the nukes we kept on site. In fact, that's always been the strongest argument for removing our weapons from Turkey. We've never been able to trust their government not to do something achingly dumb."

"Why didn't they just set up generators to keep the power running?"

"They did, but they weren't nearly as well guarded as the nuclear storage facility, so I'm sure you can guess what was targeted first. Once the generators were down… well, that was game over."

"Why? They still had to get past the guards, right?"

"Sure they did, but the folks running the heist had a huge tactical advantage. For one thing, comms were down. The Turks were flooding the frequencies used by our helmet-mounted radios, because they were trying to flush out the general and his men, so the Americans on base were on their own. Second, our boys had orders to sit back and let the Turks do their thing. Remember, this is a joint base controlled by the Turkish. The last thing we wanted to do was insert ourselves between the government and the putschists. We didn't want to accidentally shoot anyone on either side, so the American guards were ordered to stop their general patrols and withdraw to tactical locations. Their orders were to defend themselves only if someone tried to enter a US-run building, but otherwise to hold fire and let this thing play out. As a result of that order the folks running the heist faced very little resistance until they reached the nuclear storage bunker."

"And what happened when they got there?"

"Eleven dead. The theft wasn't even discovered until about three hours after they cleared out, and any trail there might have been was already stone cold by then."

"Jesus."

"Yeah," MacAuliffe sighed. "That's about the size of it. It was bad enough that it happened at all, but now... if turns out that Americans were behind this? Hell, I just don't know what to do with that. I can't imagine how– "

"Sorry, sir," the driver interrupted. "We're three minutes out."

MacAuliffe coughed and tugged on his jacket, straightening out his uniform. "Thank you, Lieutenant. Take us straight to the vehicle bay. I want to look this sonofabitch in the eye." He turned back to Jack, suddenly awkward. "Umm... I trust you understand that everything we've talked about should stay on the QT? I'm sure it'll be made public soon enough, but until then you didn't hear a word, OK?"

Jack nodded. "Understood. I don't even know how

I'd explain this to anyone."

"Explain what, Jack?" MacAuliffe gave him a wink. "We were just sitting here talking about the weather, right?"

"Yes, sir," Jack smiled, turning to gaze out the window. In the distance, from the direction of the now collapsing mushroom cloud, he could see a column of dust climb above the road for miles. From this far away the vehicles themselves were still just dark dots, but one stood out. It looked like it was a good mile ahead of the slow moving convoy, kicking up its own dust as it raced towards the base that lay ahead.

"There's our boy," MacAuliffe growled, his eyes narrowing. "Time to get some answers."

•▼•

CHAPTER THIRTEEN
MUSSOLINI'S CORPSE

LIEUTENANT RAY BIANCHI sat nervously in the driver's seat of the Jeep, clutching the wheel with clammy hands, glancing down at the bruised knuckles of his right hand with a confusing blend of fear, guilt and pride. In the seat beside him Staff Sergeant Glen Danvers looked even more nervous, and *his* bruises were even more obvious.

A black eye was blooming on his face, squeezing closed a bloodshot eye as it swelled, and dark red blood from a split lip crusted on his chin. His wrists were cuffed a little too tight behind his back, and he winced with pain whenever the Jeep hit a bump in the road. By the way he gasped his way through the potholes, Bianchi suspected he had one or two broken ribs.

Bianchi knew he'd gone too far. He knew he could have taken Danvers into custody without violence, but as soon as he received the order to place him under arrest he'd lost control. He knew he'd let his heart rule his head, and he knew he'd jumped to conclusions. But hell, it wasn't like it was a tricky conclusion to reach. It was obvious the colonel thought Danvers had something to do with the nuke.

Exactly *what* he had to do with it Bianchi couldn't guess, but what he *did* know was that Danvers had been skulking around the vehicle bay far from his assigned duties when he'd 'stumbled' on the bomb, and if the sergeant wanted to claim that was just some kinda coincidence Bianchi wasn't buying. The nuke had been hidden in a crate behind a stack of other crates.

Maybe there was some explanation that hadn't occurred to him, but if it turned out Danvers *was* involved in this mess he wanted to be able to say he'd gotten a couple of licks in before he snapped on the cuffs. He wanted to be able to boast about it, like the fierce old Italian grandmas who loved to tell people they'd spat on Mussolini's corpse in the Piazzale Loreto. His own *nonnina* had always boasted that she hit him with a rock, and the way Bianchi saw it… well, this was the same situation. Maybe it wasn't quite so clear cut, but if it turned out the way he suspected he'd be able to spend the rest of his life dining out on the story of how he split the lip of the guy who nuked America.

He just hoped he was right, because otherwise he was just a jackass who'd assaulted a fellow soldier.

In the distance the hunkered down administrative building at Beale finally came into view, and Bianchi found his foot pressing harder on the gas. He was eager to deliver Danvers. His conscience was nagging at him, and he couldn't wait for Colonel MacAuliffe to squeeze a confession out of the sergeant.

"Is there anything you want to say?" he asked, hoping that the tenth time of asking might convince Danvers to confess to him personally.

The sergeant remained stubbornly silent, staring out through the dusty windshield to the base ahead. He'd been silent ever since Bianchi pulled in front of the troop transport he'd been driving. Ever since he'd hauled him down from the cab, shoved him to the asphalt and beat seven shades out of him. Danvers had asked a few confused questions mid-beating, but as soon as Bianchi mentioned the nuke he'd clammed up and demanded to speak to a lawyer.

Since then… not a single word. He looked guilty as sin, though. Bianchi could see it in his eyes. In his body language. In the way his breathing grew a little faster as the base approached.

"Damn it, Danvers, it's obvious you were involved. Just confess!" Unconsciously he took his hand from the wheel and bunched a fist, but the only effect was to make Danvers flinch and shrink back in his seat. Still he didn't speak.

"You're gonna spend the rest of your life in a cell, you God damned traitor."

The Jeep shot through the open gates of the base, barely slowing for the guards to raise the barrier, and Bianchi smiled when he saw that the colonel had beaten them there. He was waiting beside a Humvee, smoking a cigar with what looked like a bunch of civilians and a chocolate lab.

"Time's up, Danvers," he growled, pulling the Jeep to a skidding halt in the vehicle bay. "Time to face the music."

MacAuliffe was striding over as Bianchi climbed from the car, and he'd arrived by the time he'd pulled Danvers out onto his feet. MacAuliffe frowned, chewing on his cigar as he stared at the prisoner.

"What happened to his face?" he asked, gesturing to the bruises with his cigar.

"It got a little rough, sir," Bianchi claimed, shoving the sergeant roughly up against the door. "I had to subdue him to get him in the car."

Danvers gasped with pain. He looked like he wanted to protest, but MacAuliffe spoke over him before he could get out a word. "Now, first sergeant," he said, his expression turning cold, "you and I are gonna have a little talk."

Danvers shook his head, his eyes wide. "No, sir." His voice emerged as a strained whisper.

"No, sir?" MacAuliffe took a step closer, looming over the young man. "What do you mean, no sir?"

Danvers stood to attention with great difficulty, his shoulders pulled back by the cuffs pinching his hands together behind him. "I'm sorry, sir," he said, averting his gaze as the colonel eyeballed him from just a few inches away. "I mean no offense, sir, but if I understand the situation I'm being held on suspicion of committing a crime. If that's the case I'd like to formally request counsel." He visibly shrank back as MacAuliffe's face turned a deep shade of crimson, pressing himself against the car behind him, and he continued with such little confidence that his voice was barely a whisper. "Ummm... according to the Article 31 of the Uniform Code I can't be compelled to make any statement that might lead me to incriminate myself." He coughed awkwardly. "Sir."

Bianchi scowled. The bastard was trying to worm his way out of facing the music.

"You want to lawyer up?" MacAuliffe growled.

"Yes, sir. All questioning must stop until counsel is present." Danvers looked like he was just a few seconds from wetting himself. "Those are my rights, sir."

"Those are your rights, huh?" MacAuliffe stared at him long and hard, shifting his cigar from one side of his mouth to the other, a cloud of smoke stinging Danvers' eyes. Eventually he sniffed and turned away. "Lieutenant Bianchi, hand me your sidearm."

"Yes, sir," Bianchi replied, eagerly pulling his Sig Sauer P320 from his holster and passing it to the colonel.

"Now, staff sergeant," MacAuliffe said, checking the magazine before reinserting it with a loud click. "I'm gonna make this very simple. Given the circumstances I don't think anyone would argue that I'm out of line here." He clicked off the safety. "I'm going to ask you a question, and if you don't answer in five seconds I'm going to shoot you in the leg. Is that understood, Staff Sergeant Danvers?"

"*Yessir!*" He spoke so quickly that the words blended together. His eyes bulged wide, staring at the gun. The last shred of courage floated away on the breeze.

"Good," MacAuliffe nodded. "What were you doing when you found the nuke?"

Danvers yelled out without a pause. "Sir, I was gathering medical supplies for the field hospital, sir!"

"Is that right?" MacAuliffe puffed on his cigar, holding the Sig casually in his free hand. "Your unit was assigned to construction detail on the other side of the camp. Why were you not with your unit, sergeant?"

"Sir?" Danvers couldn't take his eyes from the pistol in MacAuliffe's hand. "I… I was under orders, sir."

"You were under orders to erect tents, sergeant. Your CO is on the way here to confirm that right now."

"Yes, sir, I was, but– "

"So what were you doing in the vehicle bay, sergeant? Why were you a mile from your assigned duties rooting around the trucks?"

"Sir, I was ordered there!"

"God damn it, Danvers!" MacAuliffe raised the gun now, his voice rising. "You're gonna tell me where they put the last nuke or I swear to God I'll shoot you in the head!"

"Sir! I don't know anything about the nukes!" Danvers half collapsed against the side of the Jeep, his eyes wide and his voice breaking with terror. "I was ordered to go to that truck. The license number is in my pocket!"

Danvers flinched as Bianchi reached into the breast pocket of his jacket, pulling out a folded piece of paper. MacAuliffe snatched it from his hand and scanned the handwritten text. A license number followed by a list of medical supplies along with their crate numbers.

"What is this?" he demanded, suddenly sounding less sure of himself. He shoved the paper in the sergeant's face. "Who gave you this order?"

Danvers was sobbing now, beyond terrified. "Sir, it was General Bailey!" he cried. "General Bailey sent me there!"

•▼•

CHAPTER FOURTEEN
CASUS BELLI

GENERAL HARLAN BAILEY sat in the passenger seat of his troop truck with the relaxed, satisfied smile of a man who was seeing a lifetime of planning and years of hard work finally come to fruition. A man who'd labored long and hard, who'd risked it all, and was finally receiving the reward for his tenacity.

For the longest time he'd feared this day would never come. He'd feared it was destined to remain forever a pipe dream, an idle wish that would never come to pass, and not without good reason. The odds against it had, after all, been astronomical. Nobody would have guessed that he could pull it off.

What was happening today may seem simple enough to the uninitiated, the result of a few bombs being primed and buttons pushed, but in fact these were just the final few steps of a project that had been first set in motion a decade ago, and today's events were the result of a seed that had been planted long before that, born of a careful – ever so careful – discussion with a group of like-minded patriots.

It was an audacious plan with countless players and a million moving parts, all of which had to mesh together perfectly lest the entire thing collapse. God willing nobody outside the inner circle would ever learn all the details, but if they did they could only marvel at its intricacy. They'd be horrified, of course – Bailey was under no illusions that he'd ever be lauded for his actions – but he was equally certain they'd also be grudgingly impressed.

Despite its complexity, though, actually carrying out the plan had been the easy part. If Bailey's long, distinguished military career had taught him anything it was that a small group of well-trained, dedicated men could move mountains. The hard part had been finding the right men to move those mountains. That had proved almost impossible.

He'd always known it would be an uphill struggle, of course, but he hadn't quite understood just how difficult it would prove to endure the years of frustration, dead ends and extreme risk to secretly assemble a group of men with the skills, vision and patriotism to see the big picture. To see beyond the narrow, constrictive limits of their morality to a broader truth. In the end it had taken most of his career before he was ready to strike. Before his men were finally in position, placed in strategic positions throughout the world.

But today General Bailey knew that it had all been worth it. As he squinted in the bright sunlight to the C-130 Hercules waiting for him in the airfield ahead he knew that his long journey was almost over. Soon enough he'd be able to rest, his mission complete.

"Lower the cargo bay door, Cal."

Bailey turned to the driver beside him as the pilot called through his confirmation on the radio. On the dusty airstrip ahead the back of the C-130 split open to reveal its cavernous bay.

"Home stretch, sergeant," he said, fighting to keep the smile from his face. It didn't feel right to smile on a day like today. "How are you feeling?"

The sergeant nodded. "I'm feeling pretty damned proud, sir."

"You should, sergeant," replied Bailey, patting the man on the shoulder. "You've done your country a great service, and don't let anyone ever tell you different."

The sergeant pulled the truck behind the C-130, lining up carefully before edging forward onto the ramp. Bailey felt a rush of relief as the truck passed into the shadow of the plane, and he felt his heart beat just a little slower as the bay door began to rise. One step closer to the end.

Most people, he knew, would think him insane. *Of course* they would. He'd never been in any doubt that if his plan was ever revealed to the world he'd be cast as a monster, a traitor to the land he loved. He'd be painted as a mad man, a mass murderer, despised for all eternity by the very people he was trying to help. He understood this with a clarity only available to the sane.

But he'd made his peace with that long ago. He'd accepted that few would ever be able to understand his vision. Few would be able to see past the horror. Past the death and destruction. The years had turned them soft, idle and complacent. They wouldn't understand why they had to suffer the regrettable but necessary birthing pains of the new America.

If they learned the truth they'd never thank him for it, but all those who survived would benefit.

They'd all enjoy the riches his sacrifice would bring them, and that was enough for him. It was enough for his men, too. They understood as well as he did the burden they must shoulder. It weighed heavy, but they were patriots to a man. They wouldn't waver.

The truck trembled as the cargo bay door began to close behind them, and a moment later the cold blue bay lights flickered on as the engines began to hum to life.

Bailey felt lighter than air. He felt jubilant... ecstatic. He'd always known that the odds were stacked against him. He'd known that a thousand problems could have derailed the plan in a heartbeat, and that he'd almost certainly never reach this point. Just to be sitting there in the plane was a victory. To still be alive to witness the final strike was a triumph he'd never imagined. He forced himself to take a deep breath, to calm his nerves and still his excitement.

There *had* been problems, of course. The plan had almost failed a dozen times before, not least when the Reagan Wilkes account was discovered. If the account hadn't been frozen by that meddling DoD calculator jockey he'd have been able to secure more ships. He'd have been able to replace the freighter they lost off the Mauritania coast, and maybe even buy another for the final warhead. If he still had access to the money this could all already be over. He could have launched all nine warheads at the same moment, as planned.

But now… now he could see that if anything the change of plans had actually *helped* them. If he'd been able to follow through on his original plan San Diego and Seattle would have been leveled at the same time as the other cities. An hour of earth shattering destruction would have brought the US to its knees, but it would all have been over in an afternoon. It would have gained them nothing they didn't already have.

Destroying the safe zone hadn't been his idea, but now he wished he'd thought of it first. It was a master stroke. It offered them everything they wanted, and much more. It was… well, there were no two ways about it. It was pure, unadulterated *evil*. The emotional impact of attacking thousands of terrified fleeing refugees would aid their cause better than nuking the Statue of Liberty ten times over.

Nuking the cities had incited fear. Millions had been terrified as they fled inland. By the time Bailey gave the order to launch almost every city was near deserted, their residents running for their lives as their homes and offices were brought to the ground behind them. It was the most audacious attack in the history of terrorism, but it had *only* caused fear. Bailey needed more than that.

Bailey needed *hate*. He needed *rage*. He needed to stoke the fires of fury that would fuel America toward its next golden age, and nothing could incite hatred better than attacking refugees. Even better, it had come at almost no cost. Only a couple hundred had been killed in the attack, and the physical damage was limited to a few hundred square miles of pine forest. It was perfect.

He'd already felt the hate brewing back at the safe zone, when he'd announced the evacuation. He could see it in the eyes of the civilians as they'd crowded back into the trucks. When they'd arrived he'd only seen fear, but now… now it was simply disbelief. They were astounded by the audacity of the 'terrorists', launching an attack on innocent refugees who'd already lost their homes. As he walked toward his own truck he'd heard people pledge to get 'them' back. To destroy their homes as their own had been destroyed.

Everything was falling into place. In just a few minutes the Hercules would climb into the air and set course for the final target. The final insult. The hammer blow that would erase the last of the complacency, the sloth, and the security that had seen the country he loved rest too long on its laurels.

Soon all Americans would feel the white hot rage that would make them once again strive for greatness.

•▼•

CHAPTER FIFTEEN
STOP, DROP AND ROLL

"TED," KAREN ASKED, her voice slow and measured, as if speaking in more than a calm whisper might be enough to set it off, "why is there a nuclear bomb on the truck?"

Krasinski stared down at the open crate, his expression drawn and pale. "I, ummm…" He wiped a sheen of sweat from his forehead with a trembling hand. "Maybe they recovered it? Maybe they found it with the other one. Maybe they're… I don't know, maybe they're taking it somewhere safe."

Karen scoffed. "Come on, Ted, seriously? You think if the good guys had found it they'd send it off without any kind of escort? Think about it. If this was *us* the sky would be full of Black Hawks right now. We'd be flanked on either side by a dozen tanks. This would be the best protected vehicle on the planet. It wouldn't be driving alone down some dusty road like a damned UPS truck."

"*OK*," Krasinski hissed, stepping away from the crate. "OK, I see what you mean. Maybe we should… ummm, OK, we need to get off right now."

"Get off how?"

"*I need to get off!*" Without warning Krasinski made for the back of the truck, and it was only a moment of quick thinking from Ramos that he tripped over a stuck out foot before he leaped to his death. He tumbled to the floor of the truck, inches from the tailgate.

"OK, big guy." Ramos lowered himself beside Krasinski and held him steady as he tried to scramble away. "Let's see if we can come up with a plan that doesn't leave us all with broken necks."

"But this could go off any second now!" he protested, squirming under Ramos' grip. "We have to get away from it!"

"Ted!" Karen hissed. "Calm down. We're in the middle of nowhere. They're not going to set off a nuke just to destroy a couple of wheat fields and some telephone poles, OK? Just settle down. We have to think about this."

Valerie stared out the back of the truck with glazed eyes, seemingly hypnotized by the telephone poles whipping by at the side of the road. "I… I think we're slowing down." She tensed up, her muscles bunching. "He's right. We should get out."

Karen couldn't react quickly enough. By the time she knew what was happening Valerie was already out of reach, running at full tilt for the back of the truck. She turned to see Ramos still focused on Ted. He didn't see Valerie until she was almost past him.

"*No!*"

It happened almost too quickly to follow. Ramos reached out with his free hand to grab at Valerie's wrist, but she was moving too quickly, carrying too much momentum. She'd already launched herself towards the tailgate by the time she barreled into him, and in a split second Ramos realized he only had two options. The first was to let her go. To hope that the truck had slowed enough, and that the ground was forgiving.

He chose the second option.

With a deft flip he used Valerie's momentum against her. He didn't hold her back, but instead swung her like a pendulum back into the truck. For a moment her body was beyond the tailgate, hanging over thin air, held steady only by Ramos' tight grip on her arm, and then her feet touched down once more on the very the lip of the truck.

For a split second time and gravity seemed to hold their breath. It seemed as if they might be allowed to stay there, held in precarious balance on the edge, but the illusion only lasted for a moment. The force spent swinging Valerie back to the edge had to be balanced, and Ramos found himself hovering over the road, his weight beyond the truck. He was falling.

But he didn't fall alone. As Ramos released Valerie from his grip she reached out and took his hand once more. She knew she couldn't save him, but she couldn't let him go.

All of this happened in the blink of an eye, in the space between breaths, but by the end of it Ramos and Valerie were tumbling on the road behind the truck, rolling over and over in a cloud of dust, clutching tightly to each other as the truck peeled away.

"*Mommy!*" Emily cried from the deep shadows of the truck as Karen stepped towards the back. Karen took her by the hand and continued walking, staring wide eyed at the two figures receding into the distance. They'd come to a stop in the middle of the road, two ragged heaps on the cracked, potholed asphalt.

"Ted, can you see if they're...? Karen's voice trailed off. She wasn't sure she wanted to know the answer.

Krasinski shook his head. "I can't tell. My glasses broke in the helicopter."

Karen squinted, hoping that her vision might magically sharpen, but the distant figures had grown too small. As far as she could tell they were–

"They're moving!" Emily hopped on her feet and pointed excitedly out the back of the truck.

"Are you sure, pumpkin?" Ramos and Valerie were just hazy blobs to her eyes.

"Yeah! Doctor Ramos is waving to us!" She waved back, a grin spreading across her face. "Are we going to jump with them, mommy?"

"No!" Karen pulled Emily a little closer, as if she was worried she'd leap without thinking if her mom didn't hold her back. "It's not safe, honey. Doctor Ramos and Valerie were just very, very lucky." She looked down at Krasinski, still prone on the floor of the truck. "Ted? You're not still planning to jump, are you?"

Krasinski shook his head decisively. "That would

be a big no," he replied. "If they got away from that without any broken bones it'd be a miracle."

"Agreed. We'll wait until we're moving more slowly." She looked out at the telephone poles that ran beside the road. "Though... is it just me, or are we slowing down now?" She planted her hands on Emily's shoulders and looked her in the eye. "Pumpkin, just wait here a second. Don't go anywhere near the back, OK?"

Emily nodded. "I won't, mommy. I don't want to jump out."

Karen made her way to the tailgate, stepping over Krasinski as she went, and when she reached the edge she grabbed hold of the truck's frame and leaned around the side.

"Ted, you said this airfield was abandoned, right?"

"Yeah," Krasinski confirmed. "They haven't used it in at least five years. Not since they built the new longer strips in the west of the base."

"Well," Karen said, pulling herself back inside, "it's not abandoned today. There's a plane waiting on the runway."

"Damn it. How far away are we?"

"Maybe half a mile," Karen guessed. "Why?"

"Because we need to get out of here before anyone

comes back and finds us hanging out next to their favorite nuke. I'm guessing they wouldn't have any moral qualms about shoo– " He froze in mid-sentence, remembering that Emily was standing three feet from him. "Anyway, we don't want to be anywhere near here when someone comes to check on the cargo."

"OK, so we jump when the truck slows down." She leaned around the side once more. "I can see a couple of buildings out there. Maybe… ummm… a hundred yards or so from the plane? You think we could jump out as we pass the buildings?"

Krasinski pulled himself to his feet, joining Karen at the edge of the truck. He ducked beneath her and leaned around the side. "No," he shook his head and pointed straight ahead. "We won't pass the buildings on the way in. The road enters the airfield a few hundreds yards to the east. See that one right there?" He pointed at a tall, narrow gray concrete building. "That's the control tower. The big white block beside it is the hangar. I haven't been here in years, but if I remember correctly the parking lot is to the south of the hangar. They'll need to unload the nuke, so as soon as we're moving slowly enough we can hop out and make a run for it. We'll head straight for the hangar."

Karen pulled back from the edge and turned to Emily, kneeling down before her. "OK, pumpkin, listen. In a minute we're going to jump down onto the road, OK?"

"No!" Emily's lower lip began to wobble. "I'm too scared, mommy!"

"It's OK, honey. It's not going to be like Doctor Ramos and Valerie, OK? We'll be moving real slow when we jump, and I'll be holding you. It'll be just like jumping off the slide into the ball pit at Imagination Playhouse. Remember how you were scared to jump in when you were little, pumpkin?"

Emily nodded, wiping a tear from her cheek.

"But then remember that day you decided to be extra, *extra* brave and you jumped on that slide and went all the way down to the ball pit? Do you remember what you told me later? You said you were just scared of being scared, didn't you, pumpkin?"

Emily nodded again. "Uh huh. But mommy– "

"So I need you to be just as brave as you were back then, just this one time. Can you be extra brave for mommy?"

Emily looked down at the painted white lines whipping out behind the truck. Karen could see her reaching down within herself for ever shred of courage she could muster. "You promise it won't hurt?"

"I promise, pumpkin. Cross my heart and hope to die. I'll be holding onto you every second, OK?"

Emily sniffed and clung tight to Karen's shirt. "OK."

"Daddy will be so proud when he sees what a brave little girl you've been," she said, lifting her up beneath her arms and pulling her into a hug. "Ted? Are we close?"

Krasinski leaned back around the side, nodding. "Yeah, just a minute or so now." The truck passed a high chain link fence that stretched out into the distance, and the rumble of the tires changed as they moved from asphalt to concrete. "Get ready to jump."

He leaned back inside, gripping hold of the steel frame of the truck as he prepared for the leap. "Just a little slower. Wait until we're at walking pace. We should see the tower any sec– "

The truck suddenly veered to the left, and Karen stumbled sideways into Krasinski. "Whoa, you OK?" he asked, holding her arm until she found her feet.

"Yeah, but where are we going? I thought you said

the parking lot was near the hangar."

"It is. Look." He pointed out the back as the long white building came into view. In front of it were the white lines of a parking lot. "I don't know where we're…" He paused, listening to a sudden mechanical hum. "Oh. Oh, no."

"What?" Karen demanded. "What is it?"

Before Krasinski could answer Karen saw the problem. A shadow was cast over the truck, and with a sudden jolt it began to climb a steep incline. "What's going on?"

Beneath the tailgate the concrete vanished, replaced by the steel of a ramp, and a moment later walls appeared on either side of them.

"They're driving straight onto the plane," hissed Krasinski. "We need to get out *right now.*"

Without another word he hopped down to the ramp, but before he'd taken more than a couple of steps it began to rise from the ground with a loud mechanical whine. By the time he reached the edge it was already six feet above the concrete and still rising, and in the back of the truck Karen stood frozen, Emily in her arms. She knew she could never make it. Even as she considered jumping down the gap at the back of the plane closed to just a few feet, and then inches, and then the last narrow line of sunlight was erased with a loud thud.

The cargo bay was plunged into darkness, and the grumbling engine of the truck died away. For a moment Karen stood in an eerie silence, too afraid to breathe, holding Emily tight against her shoulder to keep her from making a sound, and then the cargo bay filled with a cold blue light. Buzzing strip lights flickered on along the walls, and somewhere off in the distance came the whir of engines.

"Ted," she whispered, so quiet she barely mouthed the words. "Get back inside!"

Krasinski froze like a deer in headlights at the sound of a door swinging open somewhere in the direction of the cockpit.

"Get us in the air, Cal." The voice echoed in the cavernous space, quickly replaced by the hiss of static from a two way radio. Another door opened with a creak, and still Krasinski stood at the back of the plane, completely exposed, visible to anyone who might glance in his direction. Karen beckoned him towards her with an urgent wave of her hand, but he seemed too afraid to move.

"Make sure she's strapped down tight, sergeant." That was the first voice, deep and booming, followed by a meek "Yes, sir."

Karen could hear movement alongside the truck. She turned her head to the left, and against the ghostly blue glow she could see a hand running along the other side of the truck's canvas covering. They were only a few seconds from emerging at the back, and when they appeared there'd be nowhere to hide. There was no way Krasinski could make it back to the truck in time now.

Karen swallowed the lump in her throat, feeling her heart pound in her chest. Ten feet. Five.

The hand stopped, bowing in the canvas, and then vanished.

"Umm, general?"

The booming voice returned, more distant now, somewhere toward the cockpit. "Yes, sergeant?"

"I just... I just want to thank you for the opportunity, sir. It's been an honor to serve with you."

Approaching footsteps echoed through the cargo bay, stopping somewhere near the cab of the truck. "Sergeant, the honor has been all mine. Sincerely." They were so close Karen could hear the rustle of their clothing as the men shook hands. "I couldn't have asked to serve with a more dedicated group of patriots, son. Your nation owes you a debt of gratitude."

At the back of the plane Krasinski finally found the courage to move. Walking on tiptoes he covered the ten yards back to the truck while the men spoke, and the deep, booming voice of what Karen guessed was an officer covered the sound of Ted's climb up to the truck. She nodded towards the dark shadows behind the crates, and with painfully slow progress they made their way to a spot that couldn't be seen from the tailgate.

Now the footsteps once again receded, and the sergeant broke into a cheerful whistle as he made his way alongside the truck. Karen sat in an awkward crouch, Emily balanced in her lap, as the man fussed over ratchet straps and kicked wooden chocks beneath the tires.

The plane began to move. Karen could feel the vibration beneath her feet, and then a slight jolt that sent her hand shooting out to find her balance on the floor.

"*What do we do?*" she desperately mouthed, staring wide eyed at Krasinski.

He didn't respond. Just a few steps away the sergeant was still ratcheting the final strap, securing the truck to the floor of the plane, his shrill whistle reaching them over the rising whine of the engines.

Karen looked to the floor, and a glint caught her eye. It was the pry bar Ramos had used to jimmy open the crates of medical supplies. An arm's length of solid steel with a wickedly sharp forked slat on the end. Even in the hands of an amateur fighter it could do some serious damage. If she could get the drop on the sergeant maybe she could—

Krasinski grabbed her arm as she reached out for it, shaking his head.

Now, finally, the sergeant was finished with his work, and Karen held herself in her painful crouch as the sound of his whistling receded towards the front of the plane. She started to move, but once again Krasinski stayed her, holding up a hand and listening intently. Finally, after an agonizingly tense minute, Karen heard the thud of a heavy door.

"He's gone," Krasinski sighed, letting out the breath he'd been holding.

Karen reached out and snatched the pry bar from the ground. "Why the hell did you stop me? We could have escaped!"

"No," Krasinski shook his head and pointed towards the back of the plane. "No, we couldn't. The cargo bay door won't open while the plane's moving on the ground. The only way to get it open is to stop the plane, and from what I can tell there are at least three people on board. Probably more. The Hercules takes a standard crew of five, and these are trained soldiers. There's no way we're beating our way past them with a metal stick."

Karen angrily dropped the pry bar, setting Emily down as she stretched out her aching legs. "Are you OK, honey?"

"What's happening, mommy? I thought we were gonna jump out."

"Yeah." Karen scanned around for some kind of solution, as if a magical escape hatch might appear in the floor. "Change of plan, pumpkin. I think we might be going for a ride."

Emily looked downcast. "But I thought we were going to see daddy. You promised. You promised before the helicopter." Her eyes welled with tears and her face flushed pink. "I…" she gasped, the tears beginning to flow. "I want to see my daddy!"

Karen grabbed her tight, pulling her in for a hug as she felt her own lip tremble. She couldn't stand to see Emily this way. "I know, pumpkin. I want to see him too. I'm so sorry."

Emily pulled away, leaving a trail of snot and tears on Karen's shoulder, and she wiped her eyes. "Can..." she sniffed, "can we call him on the phone? Can he come and pick us up?"

Karen's eyes grew wide. She couldn't believe she hadn't thought of it. "Ted! You still have your phone, right? You can call the base! Tell them to stop the plane from taking off!"

"I have it, yeah," he said, reaching into his jacket pocket and pulling out his cell. "But I don't know the phone number."

"How can you not know the number? Don't you work there?"

"No, I work at Travis AFB, and I don't know *that* number, either. Nobody calls the damned switchboard."

"So who can you call? Don't you have anything programmed in? You don't have any officer friends at Beale or... I don't know, anyone who could get a message up to someone in charge?"

Krasinski shook his head. "I have Domino's Pizza on speed dial, and the number of a private who once tried to sell me weed." He sighed, frustrated. "I'm an accountant. I'm a nobody on the base. I don't hang out with officers."

Karen pulled her own phone from her pocket, but she didn't even have to tap the screen before she knew it would be no good. The screen was shattered, and it didn't respond at all when she tried to wake it.

"Let me borrow yours," she said, snatching Krasinski's cell from his hand.

"Who are you gonna call?"

"I'm calling Jack." She fell silent for a moment, struggling to remember the number she'd long since ceded to her phone's memory rather than her own. "He was on his way to the safe zone before the bomb. Maybe he can get a message to someone."

"You're calling daddy?" Emily's face brightened, and the first hint of a smile began to creep to her lips.

"Yeah, pumpkin, I'm calling daddy. I'll let you say hello if... hang on."

She held the phone closer to her ear, struggling to hear the recorded message over a sudden roar as the plane's engines spooled up.

Sorry, this number is no longer in service.

"What the hell?" She looked down at the phone, reading the number and silently mouthing along. "Three seven four... crap, wrong number." She dialed again, praying she'd remembered it right, and as she held the phone tight against her ear she felt her heart skip a beat at the sound of ringing.

"I've got a signal!" she cried triumphantly.

Two rings.

Now three.

Five. She tensed up, remembering that the call would go to voicemail after the sixth ring.

There was a click, and a rustling sound before–

"Hello? Who's this?"

Without warning Karen felt tears stream down her face. Her voice caught in her throat.

"Jack?" her voice cracked with emotion. "Jack, honey, it's me. It's Karen."

•▼•

CHAPTER SIXTEEN
PADRON FAMILY RESERVE

STAFF SERGEANT DANVERS was almost catatonic by the time the colonel had finished with his questioning, leaning unsteadily against the Jeep, his hands trembling as he wiped tears from his cheeks. Lieutenant Bianchi fussed over him, plying him with water and trying to clean the dried blood from his face. MacAuliffe stormed off to the Humvee, swearing under his breath.

Danvers' guilt was just a misunderstanding, or at least wildly misplaced. The floodgates had burst as soon as Danvers had figured out the colonel suspected him of having something to do with the nuke. His demands for a lawyer were forgotten, and he answered MacAuliffe's questions with an eagerness that verged on mania.

The reason for the sergeant's terror, it seemed, had nothing to do with his discovery of the nuclear weapon. He and a couple of privates from Camp Roberts had stopped for a break on the way to the safe zone in the town of Lodi, California, where they'd cleaned out Stogies Cigar Lounge and ransacked a jewelers store. When they reached Truckee his unit had been assigned to construction duties on the far side of the safe zone, but Danvers had slipped away to the vehicle bay find a safe place to stash the spoils. When General Bailey found him skulking around the trucks his pockets had been weighed down by a dozen gold sovereign rings, and he was pulling three thousand dollars worth of sweat-soaked Padron Family Reserve from beneath his jacket.

Danvers had considered it a lucky escape when the general ignored the cigars. He'd been relieved when Bailey ordered him to find a specific truck and root around the back in search of a particular crate, and when Lieutenant Bianchi grabbed him from the convoy and cuffed him to the Jeep he'd assumed his crime had finally caught up with him. He'd assumed he was being taken back to Beale to be court-martialed for looting. He had no idea it was anything to do with the bomb, and no clue why the colonel was so outraged over the theft of a few boxes of cigars that he'd pulled a gun on him.

Now Danvers slumped to the ground in the shade beside the Jeep, still cuffed, but this time for a crime he'd actually committed. Meanwhile Colonel MacAuliffe stalked back and forth across the vehicle bay, watching the approaching convoy like a hawk, waiting with his weapon drawn for the general to arrive.

"You need to leave now, Jack," MacAuliffe growled, his face beetroot red as he stopped pacing for a moment. He looked about a half mile beyond furious, and ready to beat anyone who gave him a good enough excuse. "Get your people inside. This might get ugly if he's not working alone."

Jack couldn't believe what he was hearing. He couldn't believe that the colonel seemed ready to open fire on fellow American soldiers. Even if this was all true, even if General Bailey really was involved in the attacks... *Jesus*, surely it wouldn't come down to a gunfight? And surely it wouldn't all land on the colonel, his driver and Lieutenant Bianchi.

"I'm not going anywhere," he insisted. "I can

handle a gun. Just tell me where to shoot."

"Are you crazy?" MacAuliffe scoffed. "This is a military matter, Jack. You can't get caught up in the middle of this." He turned to Garside and Cathy, loitering beside the Humvee. "You and you, get inside. Jack's going with you."

Garside noticed Jack's reluctance. He didn't understand what was happening, but he'd seen the colonel threaten to kill one of his own men, and he could see that he was still agitated. "Maybe we ought to listen to the officer, Jack," he suggested. He coughed awkwardly as Jack still hesitated. "I'm sure you don't want Boomer in harm's way."

That did the trick. Jack looked down at the dog at Garside's feet, and finally his shoulders slumped. Whatever was about to happen he couldn't bear the thought of the dog being injured. Boomer had been by Jack's side ever since Seattle, and right now... well, right now the excitable mutt was his closest friend.

"OK, Doug, you win," he conceded, stepping away from MacAuliffe. "We'll go wait over in the garage. Come on, Boomer."

The dog perked up at the sound of her name, and she happily trailed along beside Jack as he headed for the enormous garage at the end of the vehicle bay.

Garside followed behind him like a sheepdog, corralling him towards the garage as if he was worried Jack might change his mind and turn back, and Cathy strode on ahead.

"What's going on with that guy?" she asked, nodding back towards MacAuliffe. "He looks like he's about to have an aneurysm."

"The colonel?" Jack shrugged evasively, wishing he could tell her what was going on. "I don't know. Something to do with looting, I think. He has to arrest one of his men." He felt awful for lying to her, but he'd promised the colonel.

"Looting?" Cathy shook her head with disgust. "Damn, as if we don't have enough problems to deal with. You'd think soldiers would know better."

You don't know the half of it, Jack thought, looking back to the convoy of trucks beginning to crawl onto the base. He picked up his pace a little, determined to make it to the garage before General Bailey's truck rolled into the bay. He knew a raging gunfight was unlikely, but still he felt a little too exposed out on open ground. He wanted to–

He froze. Something was vibrating in his pocket, and it wasn't until he reached in and pulled it out that he realized it was his phone. It felt like weeks since he'd received a call.

One bar.

Unknown caller.

"Guys, hang on a second, someone's calling me."

Cathy stopped, pulling out her own phone. "Wow, you have a signal? Hot damn."

Jack felt his heart skip a beat as he tapped the screen and brought the phone to his ear. He didn't want to get his hopes up, but…

"Hello? Who's this?"

The speaker crackled in his ear. The signal was so weak it was barely there, but over a loud, constant hum he heard a sharp sob.

"Jack? Jack, honey, it's me. It's Karen."

For what felt like an eternity he couldn't speak. The words wouldn't come. His head span, but eventually a broad smile spread across his face and he let out a joyous laugh.

"*Karen!* Oh my God, you're alive!" He was almost yelling into the phone, unable to control the volume of his own voice. "Are you OK? Is Emily with you?"

"Yes, she's with me." Karen's voice wobbled as she fought past tears. "We're both OK, honey, but look, I don't have much time, and I need you listen very closely."

Jack's breath caught in his throat. "I'm listening," he croaked, overcome by a sudden sense of dread. *What's wrong?*

"We're on an airplane. A..." her voice faded for a moment as she mumbled to someone in the background. "A C-130 Hercules. We're at an airfield near Beale Air Force Base, honey. That's west of the safe zone, on the way to Yuba City."

"I'm at Beale right now!" Jack spun around as if he might be able to see the plane. "I can come find you!"

"No, honey, you can't. Just listen, OK? We're on the runway and we're about to take off. The people flying the plane don't know we're here." For a moment she fell silent. Jack wanted to speak desperately, but there was something about the tone of the silence that made him hold his tongue.

"Honey, there's a nuclear bomb on the plane."

Jack's blood froze in his veins, and the hairs on the back of his neck stood on end. "There's a bomb on the plane?" he repeated in leaden tones.

"Jack, I need you to find someone in charge. I need you to explain what's going on. I think they're planning to drop the bomb somewhere." She paused for a moment, steeling herself. "And Jack. I think the people with the bomb are Americans."

Jack was already at a dead run, the phone still pinned to his ear as he sprinted back towards Colonel MacAuliffe. "Hang on, just stay on the line," he panted. "I'm passing you to someone."

Jack broke his run against the hood of the Jeep, gasping for breath as MacAuliffe turned and stared at him.

"I thought I told you to get out of here, son," the colonel complained.

"No," Jack gasped, cursing his lack of fitness as he held up his phone. "You need to hear this. My wife's on the line."

"Your wife? Why the hell would I need to speak to your wife?"

"Just listen," he impatiently ordered, turning on the speaker and setting the volume higher. "Honey, you're on with Colonel MacAuliffe. He's in charge here. Tell him what you just told me."

"MacAuliffe?" This time the voice belonged to a man. "I was trying to get hold of that asshole all night!"

The colonel bristled at the insult. "I don't know who this is, but you should know you're on speaker. This is MacAuliffe."

"And I'm sure I'll be mortified when this is all over,

colonel, but we'll have to save the apology for later. This is Ted Krasinski. I'm DoD, based out of Travis."

"What's this about, Krasinski?" MacAuliffe demanded. "We're a little busy here."

"Colonel, right now you have a C-130 preparing for takeoff on the old airfield in the south east quadrant of Beale. In the cargo bay is a truck that broke away from a convoy headed back from Truckee, and in the back of that truck is a nuclear warhead."

MacAuliffe's expression didn't flicker as he heard the news. "Understood. Is General Bailey on board?"

"Bailey? Are you talking about Harlan Bailey?"

"Yes, son. Is he on the plane?"

"I… I don't know, sir, but I heard one guy refer to someone as a general. Deep voice? Kind of a southern drawl?"

"That sounds like Bailey," MacAuliffe nodded. "Son, I need you to get off that plane right now, y'hear?"

"I don't think that's possible, sir. We're stuck in the cargo bay. The bay door won't open while the plane is rolling, but if you have any suggestions I'm all ears."

The colonel scratched his stubble, swearing under his breath. "Is there any way you'd be able to disrupt the takeoff? Could you take the plane?"

"I don't know how I could possibly do that, sir."

"You're DoD? Don't you have any combat training?"

"Ummm, no sir. I'm an accountant." In the background the engines built to a roar. "I think we're picking up speed now, sir. Do you know how I could kill this thing from the cargo bay?"

MacAuliffe scratched his stubble, deep in thought. "Have you tried the emergency doors? That should set off a cockpit alarm. They'll have to abort the takeoff."

"Emergency doors? Where can I find them?"

"You'll see them port and starboard, just in front of the cargo ramp. Pull down on the release handle and the door should open outwards."

"OK, I'm checking it now." A muffled rustle came from the speaker as Krasinski climbed down from the truck.

"Son, you need to be ready to run as soon as those doors open, OK? These guys will come out all guns blazing when they realize you're on their plane."

"Understood, sir," Krasinski replied. "We're ready. Hang on." More rustling, and after a few moments Jack heard him swear under his breath. "Sir, it looks like these doors have been sealed shut. I can see weld marks all around the frame."

"Damn it," MacAuliffe cursed. "He's using a boneyard plane." He noticed Jack's questioning look. "Decommissioned. They weld the doors to prevent theft." He turned back to the phone. "OK son, do you see anything around you that you could use to prevent takeoff? Anything at all. Even if it's just a bunch of exposed wires you could tug out of the wall?"

There was a moment's pause before Krasinski's voice returned. "No sir, I don't see anything. It's pretty bare in here. The only thing I can see is a parachute hanging on the wall."

MacAuliffe's eyes flickered to Jack for a moment, and then down to the ground. He seemed to have something to say, but he was reluctant to say it.

"Son," he finally muttered. "If you can't keep that plane on the ground you understand what needs to happen?"

There was a long silence before Krasinski answered. "Yes, sir," he replied, his voice almost a whisper. "I know what you have to do."

Jack felt his stomach turn over. "What? What do you have to do?"

"Godspeed, Krasinski," MacAuliffe said. "We're gonna stay on the line until we lose you, OK?"

"Colonel, what do you have to do?" He felt sick. "Karen, what's happening?"

"I… we're taking off," Karen replied. "Ted, what's going on?"

For a moment nobody spoke. The only sound was the rising whine of the engines as the Hercules powered along the runway, and a crackle in the line as it moved to the limits of the local cell tower. Finally MacAuliffe sighed.

"We have to shoot it down, Jack."

Jack felt his fists clench and his jaw set. "My wife and daughter are on that plane!"

"*Daddy!*" Emily's voice rang out across the vehicle bay. Jack grabbed the phone from the hood of the Jeep and held it close.

"Pumpkin!" he cried, trying to keep the fear and anger from his voice. "I'm so happy to hear you. I love you so, so much."

"I love you, daddy," she cried over the roar of the engines. "When are you coming to get us?"

Jack looked up to see MacAuliffe walking away toward the arriving convoy. "I'm coming soon, pumpkin. We'll all be together soon, OK?" He wiped a tear from his cheek. "Karen, are you there?"

"I'm here." Karen couldn't keep the tears from her voice. It trembled as she spoke. "I love you, Jack."

"I'm not going to let this happen, Karen. I'm going to stop it, OK?"

Karen's voice was almost gone now, crackling as it faded. "Honey, listen. We left Doc Ramos and his friend behind on the road to the airfield. They could be injured. You have to promise me you'll find them, OK?"

"I promise, Karen. They'll be here when you get back, I promise."

"Jack, I wish we could– "

With a final crackle the call dropped, and Jack held the phone to his chest as if he were holding Karen and Emily themselves.

"Colonel!" he yelled. "You can't do this!" He slipped the phone back into his pocket and followed MacAuliffe toward the convoy. "Colonel!"

"I'm sorry, Jack." MacAuliffe broke off from giving orders to a handful of men climbing down from the back of a truck. "I really am sorry, but I can't let Bailey get away with that bomb. I can't sacrifice thousands of people just for the sake of your wife and dau– "

He didn't see the punch coming. It was a wild, clumsy left hook, but it caught MacAuliffe on the jaw and sent him staggering back against the truck. Jack hadn't thrown a real punch since high school. There wasn't enough force behind it to deal any serious damage, but as MacAuliffe recovered he wiped blood from a split lower lip.

"Under the circumstances I'm gonna let that slide, Jack," he muttered, spitting a gob of blood to the ground. "But I'm warning you, if you ever– "

He saw the second swing from a mile away. Jack telegraphed it like an amateur after a dozen beers, dipping his shoulder as he drew back his fist, and MacAuliffe deftly sidestepped. Jack's fist sailed through thin air, and before he knew what was happening he met an upper cut coming the other way. His head rocked back, and before he had the time to recover – before he even had time to feel any pain – a neat, efficient jab flattened his nose against his face. He stumbled back two steps before tripping over his heels, landing in the dirt with a thud.

"You only get one free shot, Jack." MacAuliffe growled. "Bianchi, cuff him."

Lieutenant Bianchi took a hesitant step forward. "Sir? Ummm, I'm sorry sir, but I only have the one set of cuffs, and… well, Sergeant Danvers is already in them."

MacAuliffe sighed. "Then… Oh, I don't know. Just get him the hell away from me."

Jack lay dazed on the ground, his ears ringing, and he didn't fight back as Bianchi took his arms and dragged him away from the colonel. Bianchi hauled him back to the Jeep, bundled him against the door beside Danvers and gave him a stern warning to stay put. In the background he could hear MacAuliffe continue to yell orders, his voice growing angrier by the second.

"OK, I want two Eagles deployed ASAP, and I want my radar up and running five minutes ago."

Jack heard mumbling, though he couldn't make out the words.

"What do you mean, they're not fueled?"

More mumbling.

"Well, where the hell are my ground crew? We need those planes in the air! No, seventy five minutes is not acceptable, captain!"

Jack's mind was full of cotton wool, still recovering from the blows. He could feel his nose throbbing, and his upper lip was wet with blood. He was certain the nose was broken, and when he saw the colonel storm around the side of the Jeep he shrank back, expecting another punch. Instead MacAuliffe dropped to his haunches and plunged his hand into Jack's pocket, pulling out his phone.

"You're one lucky sonofabitch, Jack," he growled, tapping the screen as he spoke. "Looks like you got your wish." He stared at the screen, whispering to himself. "Come on, come on, *send*, damn it."

After a few moments MacAuliffe tossed the phone into Jack's lap, turned back towards the truck and called out. "I want a Chinook ready to go right this Goddamn second, understand? Get to it!"

Jack blinked away tears and reached down for the phone. The screen was cracked and half obscured by dust, but he could see the notification still hanging on the screen.

Message delivered

He tapped through to his messages and selected the sent folder. When the words flashed across the screen a grin slipped onto his bruised face.

"Well?" MacAuliffe turned back to the Jeep with a sigh. "I'm not waiting for your sorry ass all day. Are you coming or staying?"

•▼•

CHAPTER SEVENTEEN
WORLD WAR III

KAREN SAT CLUTCHING Ted's phone long after the call had disconnected, staring at the signal bars as they fell to zero, and when the final bar blinked out she felt her heart sink. She couldn't believe what she'd just heard.

"He has no choice," Krasinski eventually muttered, breaking the heavy silence. "He can't let them drop the bomb."

"Jack said he'd stop him," whispered Karen, her voice hoarse. "He said he'd save us." She knew the idea was ridiculous. She knew Jack couldn't possibly stop the colonel from shooting down the plane, but she couldn't help but cling on to that last shred of hope, no matter how tenuous her grip.

"There's nothing he can do." Krasinski shook his head sadly, his head slumped between his knees. "MacAuliffe will launch... well, I guess he'll launch fighters. Beale's mostly on UAVs now, but they've probably still got a few jets on standby. I'd say we've got..." He glanced at his watch. "I don't know, maybe twenty minutes, a half hour? Enough time to... you know, prepare ourselves, I guess. Get our heads right."

Karen stared at him through tear filled eyes, hugging Emily tight against her chest. "How can you be so calm about this? They're going to..." She stopped when she noticed Emily looking up at her. "How are you not going crazy?"

"Oh, I am," replied Ted. "I've never been so scared, but at least..." He sighed. "Hell, at least we know it's not all for nothing, right? I mean, think about it. They only know about the bomb because we told them. They bring this thing down and we save thousands of lives. Hundreds of thousands, maybe. *And* they get the bastard who's running the show. That's... I don't know. I just never thought I'd get the chance to go out a hero, know what I mean?"

Karen wiped her eyes. "I wish I had your outlook, Ted."

Krasinski gave her a weak smile. "Well, I'm an accountant. Pretty much the best case scenario for someone like me is a heart attack on a golf cart in Florida. At least this way I might get a Ted Krasinski Day or something. And you can have a Karen… sorry, I forgot your last name."

"Archer." She sniffed. "It's Karen Archer. And Emily Archer. We can share a day."

Emily looked up at Karen. "Mommy, you said it was Keane now. When Miss Jessop calls out the register she says Emily Keane."

Karen squeezed Emily tight. "Forget that, pumpkin. I was being stupid. You're Emily Archer, just like daddy, OK?"

"OK," she smiled. "I always liked Archer better than Keane anyway. When I get back to school can I ask Miss Jessop to change the register?"

Karen couldn't help but let a sob escape her lips, and she pulled Emily close until she started to squirm in her arms.

"Mommy, you're squeezing my tummy."

"Sorry, pumpkin," Karen managed to whisper, sniffing away her tears. "First thing when we get home we'll go straight to Miss Jessop and ask her to change it, and daddy can come with us too. Does that sound good?"

"Really?" Emily nodded, grinning. "Can I show daddy my new thing?" She grabbed the bright red tie Valerie had given her back at the bus.

"I'm sure he'll think it's beautiful, pumpkin," Karen smiled. She pulled Emily closer and looked back at Ted, lowering her voice. "Will it hurt?"

He shook his head. "I don't think so. It'll be over quick. If we're lucky we won't even know it happened. We'll just... not be here any more."

It was clear from the tone of his voice that he didn't believe what he was saying, but Karen appreciated the lie. She squeezed Emily a little closer.

"I don't want her to feel anything." She took a shuddering breath, closing her eyes for a few moments as she tried to calm herself, but she felt her fear give way to anger. "I just wish we knew *why* this was happening. Why are they doing this to us?"

Krasinski nodded thoughtfully. He reached into his jacket and pulled out his pill case, popping a tablet from it and offering it to Karen. She shook her head, and he flicked the pill onto his tongue.

"I think I may have an idea," he said, swallowing the Xanax.

"An idea about what?"

"About why this is happening." He paused, easing the pill down his dry throat. "It's just a theory. I could be way off, but that name..." He ruffled his fingers through what was left of his hair and leaned back against the wall of the truck, waiting for the pill to take effect. "The colonel said it was General Harlan Bailey, and unless there are two of them..."

He shook his head. "Bailey was... well, he was a legend. Marine Corps pilot, decorated out the ass. This guy won the Medal of Honor back in Desert Storm, two weeks into his first tour of duty. He punched out over Basra when his Harrier got hit by a SAM, and the way I heard it he had a clear run back to safety. He could have made it to the border with a half day hike across friendly territory, but instead he turned and walked in the other direction. He got himself intentionally captured by the Republican Guard, then after two months chained to a wall in some godforsaken Iraqi jail he staged a prison break and took a half dozen British POWs over the border *on foot*. We're talking about a serious badass here."

Karen shook her head, confused. "What does this have to do with anything, Ted?"

"I'm just trying to tell you this guy was, y'know, a real Captain America type. He saw action in pretty every campaign for twenty years. The guy bled red, white and blue. Probably would have made it to general five years sooner if he'd sat his ass behind a desk and played the game, but he didn't want to leave his men behind." It was clear from Krasinski's tone that he had a lot of admiration for the man.

"Then about ten years ago they finally managed to chain him to a desk. I heard they made him Deputy Director of Ops at the US European Command or something." Krasinski slid back against the wall of the truck as the Xanax finally kicked in, the lines melting from his face.

"Apparently he went a little weird once he was staring an office in the face every day. Tried to get himself bumped down to lieutenant colonel a couple of times, hoping they might let him go back to the field, but they turned him down. I think they thought he'd seen too much, y'know? Like, maybe they were worried he'd end up going all Colonel Kurtz if they sent him back out into the world." He paused, staring down at Karen's phone beside her. The screen had lit up, and it hummed as it vibrated across the steel floor of the truck. "Is that a call?"

Karen snatched up the phone and tapped the screen. "No, it's a message. Looks like I got a bar again for a few seconds."

"Really? We must have caught another cell tower. Are you still getting a signal?"

Karen didn't answer. As the message appeared on the screen her brow knitted in confusion, and a moment later Krasinski jumped as she squealed with excitement.

"Look!" She thrust the phone towards him. "It's from Jack!"

He squinted at the screen, and as they came into focus he slumped back against the wall of the truck, his muscles turning to jelly as the tension flowed from his body.

Can't launch pursuit. Up to you. Destroy bomb or take plane. Good luck.

"Are you sure that's from Jack? Sounds more like the colonel to me." He waved away the thought. "What am I saying? Who gives a damn who sent it? They're not shooting us down!" He suddenly leaped to his feet, energized by the news. "We're not gonna die! OK. OK. We, ummm…" He hurried around the truck, flipping crate lids as he moved. "We need to come up with some kind of plan. We need weapons ready when this thing lands."

"Ted!" Karen hissed impatiently. "Maybe stop jumping around so close to the nuclear weapon?" She lowered her voice and tried to speak in a calming tone. "Look, let's... let's just take our time. I don't want to go off half cocked here. Sit down and let's try to think calmly about it, OK?

"Sorry, yeah." Krasinski took a deep breath and forced himself to sit, struggling to focus. His eyes were so wide they seemed to pop from their sockets, as if he'd just shotgunned a keg of energy drinks. Karen felt the same way, but she knew that neither of them would be any good in this state. They'd make mistakes, and those mistakes would screw up the reprieve they'd just been given.

"OK, why don't you keep going with your story, Ted?" she suggested.

"You can sit still and listen to a story *now*?" Krasinski was incredulous. "Seriously?"

Karen closed her eyes, focusing on her breathing. "Doesn't matter if you tell the story or sing Jimmy Crack Corn. We just need to take a minute to clear our heads before we come up with a plan. It's the time that's important, not the words."

Krasinski shook his head in disbelief as Karen

crossed her legs and began to take slow, deep breaths. "OK, fine," he sighed. "Where was I?"

Karen replied slowly, without opening her eyes. "Some hotshot general wanted to go back into the field, but they wouldn't let him."

"Oh yeah, right. Well, in the end Bailey wrote this book. *From the Ashes*, I think it was called. A serving general would usually have his manuscript snapped up in minutes, but when he shopped it around the big publishers none of them bit, then the smaller houses turned him away. Apparently it was a little too off the wall for anyone to touch. *Nobody* wanted their name attached to this thing. Word got out that he'd written this weird, rambling manifesto full of lunatic ideas about the nature of war, and when a couple of chapters were leaked to the press people started talking about it so much that Bailey eventually self published the thing."

"Yeah," Karen nodded, a faint memory creeping into her mind. "I think I read about that on Facebook. Wasn't there some big petition to get him fired?"

"Yeah. Well, dishonorably discharged," Krasinski corrected. "This book was... well, it was just *weird*. Five hundred pages of stream of consciousness nonsense and crazy rants about everything from the space program to GMOs to climate change. It read as if someone had transcribed the thoughts of a drunk lunatic. At first a lot of people thought some crazy conspiracy theorist was just using Bailey's name, but then the general came out and claimed the thing as his own. Said he stood by every word."

Karen dredged through her memory. "Didn't he claim that vaccines were making our soldiers weaker? Something about how we were letting too many kids with weak immune systems survive to adulthood?"

"Oh yeah, that one made a lot of people mad," Krasinski nodded. "But most people only picked up on the really crazy fringe stuff he was talking about. They focused on the weird clickbait craziness about vaccines and chemicals in the water, because that stuff was so wrong it was funny, but they pretty much ignored his central thesis. *That* was the really crazy thing."

"What was it? I never read the book."

"No, neither did most people. If they had they may not have laughed at him so hard. See, Bailey fancied himself a bit of a historian. He never formally studied it, but he was *obsessed* with accounts of World War II. The book was riddled with quotes from US officers, British conscripts, German politicians, Japanese businessmen... He must have read every book ever written about the war, from every perspective, and when he came to write his own book he thought he'd got it all figured out."

Krasinski realized he'd been idly tapping the crate beside him, and when he remembered it contained the nuke he snatched his hand away as if he'd touched a hot plate.

"What he decided was that the war was the best thing that ever happened to the human race. He thought there was nothing in the history of humanity that had driven us forward so far and so fast. No single event – no entire *century*, for that matter – in which we achieved as much as we did over those years."

Karen opened one eye. "That seems a little insensitive. I'm guessing he didn't have many Jewish friends."

Krasinski waved his hand dismissively. "Sure, but that's not the crazy thing. Once you strip away all the death and terrible ideologies it's a pretty common belief among historians that the war was *objectively* positive, no matter how gruesome that may sound. As far as technology was concerned the war *was* the greatest leap forward we ever made. Necessity is the mother of invention, after all. It drove the kind of innovation that took us to the moon a couple of decades later – hell, NASA hired a bunch of Nazi rocket scientists – and entire industries were created from advances made during the war. You wouldn't have that phone in your hand if it hadn't happened, and it'd probably still take two days to download a song from the Internet if we hadn't made such massive strides in computing back then."

"Even so..."

"And then there's the economic surge of the war, along with its aftermath. You look at Japan and Germany, at the Marshall Plan and Japanese economic reform. You look at the rise of the American middle class on the back of industrial growth, the economy doubling, *tripling* in size in just a couple of decades. It can't be denied that the war was the trigger for a great surge forward for humanity."

Karen frowned. "OK, fine. So if we're assuming that millions of deaths were a good trade for the moon landing and faster internet, what did he say that was so crazy?"

"The crazy thing," Krasinski replied, "was that

General Bailey suggested we should do it again."

"What, have a war?"

"Not just *a* war. We go to war all the time. He suggested we have another *world* war. Another massive global conflict that kills millions. What's more, he suggested that we should start it *intentionally*. He said that generations of peace had made us complacent and lazy. He said we'd lost our drive to innovate, to push ourselves forward, and he thought we needed the genuine threat of annihilation to spur us on. I remember he likened it to throwing a kid into a pool. He said if we weren't faced with that sink or swim test we'd never dare get our feet wet."

Now Karen opened both eyes. "That's... that's not just crazy. That's stupid."

Krasinski nodded. "Well, yeah, I agree, and so did almost everyone else. That's why *From the Ashes* was pulled from sale. The Marine Corps didn't want one of their most respected generals within a million miles of the idea that we start World War Three. That kinda talk would be catnip for the anti-war crowd, and since he was still in uniform they had the final say on whether he could publish. The book was pulled about two weeks after it went on sale, but by then it had already sold about twenty thousand copies."

"I never heard about any of the war stuff. Did it make the news?"

Krasinski shook his head. "No, the Marine Corps were happy to keep the attention on the crazy clickbait. Word is they actually *encouraged* the weird stories about vaccines and climate change to keep people distracted from what Bailey was actually suggesting, because they figured it was better to have people think he was just a little crazy than actually evil."

"So how come they didn't just discharge him? Why keep him around if he was obviously insane?"

Krasinski shrugged. "Bailey was a popular officer. He was a *bona fide* war hero with a Medal of Honor hanging around his neck. They didn't want to stand by his beliefs but they didn't want to throw him to the dogs, so instead of discharging him they sideways promoted him to some do nothing admin post at Parris Island back in South Carolina. They figured he could keep his head down a couple of years. Y'know, just stay quiet until it was time for him to retire honorably."

"And now you're thinking he wasn't just speaking hypothetically? You think he's actually trying to start a war? You think this is the guy sitting up in the cockpit right now?"

Krasinski shrugged. "It's just a theory, but... well, it certainly looks that way, yeah. Unless there are two generals named Harlan Bailey."

"But what about the people with him? Surely it's not possible to pull off something like this with just a couple of guys, right?"

"Well, that's the thing," Krasinski replied. "Once the rush to condemn Bailey started to die down something else took its place. Forums started to pop up all across the Internet full of people who thought the idea had merit. Turns out there's this entire subculture of folks who think that what we really need is a good war. They see the country as hopelessly divided, bickering over petty grievances and nonsense identity politics. They think we're stagnating and navel gazing while nations like China threaten to overtake us as the dominant global force."

A memory came to Karen, some half remembered post she'd seen in amongst the endless Minions memes that filled her Facebook feed. "Are you talking about the Year Zero thing?"

"You've heard of it?"

"Not really. I've seen a couple of friends post some

stuff, but I don't usually click on the political articles. I don't have time to worry about that kind of thing."

"Well, yeah, that's it. Year Zero is what they called the movement. Well, I say *movement*, but I always assumed it was just a bunch of misanthropic weirdos in their parents' basements. I guess they're kinda like an offshoot of the prepper movement, but these folks aren't just *preparing* for disasters but encouraging them."

"And you think Bailey managed to find people who believed in it so much they'd actually help him out?"

Krasinski gestured to the crate beside him. "It damned sure looks like he did, yeah."

"But who could be so crazy they'd listen to this guy?"

Krasinski shrugged. "People listen to all sorts of things we think are crazy. Hell, my neighbor back home tried to sell me on the flat earth theory a couple of months ago, and that's insane. At least this thing has... well, at least there's some logical consistency to it. Wanting to kill millions of people just so we can kickstart the economy and finally invent the technology behind a working hoverboard sounds dumb to me, but the thing is it would probably work. It's God damned abhorrent, but I can understand why people might find it an attractive prospect."

Karen sighed. "OK, so this guy wants to scapegoat Russia, right? That's how he plans to start his war?"

"As far as I can tell, yeah. All of the ships he used have links back to Moscow. It's a pretty safe bet that he's hoping we make the connection."

"But people will see through it, right? Surely it's not enough to just point to a stack of ship registrations and jump to the conclusion that the Russians did it. That's... that's like the first half of a Scooby Doo cartoon. We'd have to be dumb as rocks not to pull off the fake Stalin mustache and see that it was old man Bailey all along."

"It sounds dumb to us, yeah," Krasinski agreed, "but if you don't think that'll be enough you don't know people. This isn't a courtroom. Bailey doesn't need to present an airtight case. All he has to do is form the right *narrative*. It's about writing a story that makes sense to people, not selling them on every detail. Hell, pretty much every work of fiction ever written would fall apart if you pull on the wrong thread."

"But this is– "

"Trust me, Karen" Krasinski interrupted. "That will be enough. You get some anchorman to flash a couple of documents with Cyrillic writing on Joe Sixpack's TV and he's sold, even if the rest of the evidence is paper thin. Even if the Russians scream at the top of their voice that they had nothing to do with it, Joe Sixpack will still believe they did it. In fact he'll believe it even more."

"Why?"

"Because the easiest lie you'll ever tell is that lie people already want to believe, and Americans have never had a problem believing that Russians are the bad guys. It's in our DNA. On some level we've always seen them as the enemy. That's the narrative we recognize. It's something we've always wanted to believe, and we only need the slightest push to turn that belief into unimpeachable truth."

So what, you think we'll really go to war over this?"

"I really, honestly do. Right now in Washington the phones will be ringing off the hook with people demanding that we hit back at someone, *anyone*. We need to. It's not in our nature to be victims. The country simply won't tolerate us not getting our righteous revenge. The Japanese hit Pearl Harbor on

December 7th 1941. Do you remember the date we declared war on them?" He paused for a beat. "It was December 8th, and there were probably more than a few people asking why we waited so long."

He sighed. "So yeah, I'm guessing that people will already be following the breadcrumb trail. The name of the Nakharov has been public for a whole day now, and right about now some shiny haired news anchor will be talking about how it was owned by a shady Moscow shell. Soon enough everyone in the US will *know* that this was the fault of the Russians."

"And then that's it. That's the ball game. We'll *have* to strike back. God willing it won't be nuclear, but we'll have no choice but to do *something*, and once we do there'll be no way to put the toothpaste back in the tube. Once the first shot has been fired it won't even matter if we finally figure out that Bailey was behind it, because events will have overtaken us."

"OK, so how do we stop it?"

"The only way is to stop that first shot." He reached inside his torn corduroy jacket and withdrew a manila envelope. "It sounded like Colonel MacAuliffe already knows the truth, or at least suspects it, but he's still in the satellite blackout zone so we can't rely on him to get his information back to

Washington. We need to expose Bailey ourselves. We need every man, woman and child in the country to know right now that this has nothing to do with any foreign power."

"And how can we do that from up here? Does anyone on the ground have the evidence?"

Krasinski shook his head. "No. I filed my report on the Reagan Wilkes account a few days ago, but it'll be months before anyone bothers to read it. By then it won't matter."

"So what can we do?"

Krasinski frowned, holding up the envelope. "We have to get this to the ground. We need to get it somewhere that has a direct line to the White House."

Karen took a deep breath. "OK. OK... so what, we just wait for this thing to land and then try to sneak off before anyone sees us?"

"No." Krasinski shook his head. He pulled himself to his feet, turned and looked down at the nuclear warhead in the crate. "First we need to do something about this."

•▼•

CHAPTER EIGHTEEN
SCARED OF HEIGHTS

JACK HELD ON for dear life to the plastic seats that lined each wall of the Chinook, staring wide eyed out the rear door at the ground that – somehow – was directly beneath them. He felt as if he'd tumble out of the helicopter if he loosened his grip for so much as a second.

"Are they gonna close that?" he yelled, pointing to the ramp that opened out over clear space.

"What?" Colonel MacAuliffe turned to him impatiently, annoyed by the distraction.

"I said are they gonna– "

MacAuliffe shook his head and reached over Jack's shoulder, pulling a set of ear protectors from a hook on the side wall. He leaned in and raised his voice "Speak into the mic, Jack. We don't wear these things to keep our ears warm."

Jack pulled on the headset, and immediately the deafening thud of the rotor was muffled to near silence. He pulled the mic close to his mouth and yelled again. "The door! Will they close the door?"

MacAuliffe looked back at the open bay door and smiled. Far below the buildings of the airbase looked like some kind of toy town. "You scared of heights or something, Jack?" The voice sounded mocking in his ears.

"No, I'm not scared of…" He stopped, realizing it was stupid to lie for the sake of dumb pride. "Oh, screw it. *Yes*, I'm scared of heights. I had to jump out of a plane yesterday, colonel. Could you please ask someone to close the door?"

MacAuliffe laughed, reaching through to the cockpit to tap the pilot on the shoulder. A few moments later the bay door began to ascend, and Jack let out a sigh of relief when it finally closed with a heavy thud. "I hope your wife has bigger balls than you, Jack."

"What do you mean?"

"I mean that we're relying on her and her accountant buddy to get us out of this mess. The Chinook tops out at around two hundred miles per hour, but the Hercules can cruise at more than three hundred. If Bailey isn't planning to set her down there's no way we're catching up to him, and our Eagles won't be in the air for another hour or so. It's up to your girl to stop that bastard from dropping his last nuke, and when the moment comes to act I hope she doesn't clam up and complain about the damned view."

Jack leaned in, ignoring the insult. "So what are we doing in the air if we can't catch them? Why bother chasing?"

"We're not chasing the plane, Jack," the colonel replied. "If I'm reading the radar screen right, Bailey's headed on a direct course to Vegas. Bastard probably wants to see the Bellagio go up in a mushroom cloud, but we're not gonna let him. Unless your girl and her buddy manage to take control of that plane, the moment we're in range I'm going to order it shot down."

"In range of what?" Jack was confused. "I thought you said you couldn't catch up with them."

"We can't, but Nellis can take them out with a surface to air missile."

Jack's heart sank. He'd thought Karen was safe from this. "Nellis?"

"Nellis Air Force Base, Jack. Outside of Vegas. We'll be in radio range in about a half hour, and as soon as we make contact I'm ordering them to use a Patriot missile to knock that bastard out of the sky. I just pray that we manage to make contact before they reach the city."

"With all due respect, colonel," Jack growled, "I hope we don't."

MacAuliffe studied Jack, taking in the crooked nose, the purple bruises forming around his eyes and the dried blood crusted on his upper lip, and he sighed. "Look, I'm sorry about hitting you, Jack. I understand why you'd wanna take a swing at me. I'd do exactly the same if I were in your position, but that doesn't change anything. That plane has to come down before it reaches the city. I don't expect it to make you feel any better, but there are lots of wives and daughters sitting in Vegas right now."

"Yeah," Jack conceded with an angry sigh, leaning back in his seat, "but they're not mine."

MacAuliffe set a comforting hand on Jack's shoulder. "Well, like I said, I hope your wife has a set of balls. If she can take that plane we can all go home heroes. I'll pin the medal on her myself."

"Take the plane?" Jack shook his head,

incredulous. "She's got courage, colonel, much more than I do, but she's an office supply manager and a mom. She's not John Rambo. What exactly do you expect her to do?"

MacAuliffe shrugged. "I don't know, Jack, but like you said, she's a mom. I've fought in honest to God wars, and I can tell you that I'd rather be airdropped naked in the middle of a Kandahar firefight than stand between a mom and her daughter. People don't know what they're capable of until their kids are in danger. I'm guessing you know that better than most, right?"

Jack scowled. He hated to admit it, but he knew MacAuliffe was right. In the last couple of days Jack had done things he could barely believe, all in the name of getting back to his little girl. Hell, he'd jumped out of a plane. He'd buried two people, and not ten minutes ago he'd taken a swing at a damned Air Force colonel.

If he could do all that then maybe... maybe it wasn't beyond hope. Maybe Karen could find some way to take control of the plane.

He turned away from MacAuliffe and looked out the circular window in the side of the Chinook. Far below them the pine forests of the Sierra Nevadas were giving way to the arid badlands of Nevada, green shifting into red, orange and brown. Somewhere far ahead of them the Hercules was widening the gap, moving towards Vegas a mile a minute faster than the Chinook, and he knew that whatever happened from here that plane would be on the ground in about a half hour, either blown apart by a Patriot missile, vaporized in a massive mushroom cloud or maybe, just maybe, sitting on a runway with Karen and Emily safe.

He looked up to the sky, closed his eyes and began to whisper a prayer.

•▼•

CHAPTER NINETEEN
THE LOADMASTER'S CHUTE

KAREN LEANED WARILY over the crate, peering down at the nuclear warhead within. She'd expected to be gripped by an unspeakable terror at the sight of the bomb just inches from her face. She'd expected to be frozen, panicked and struck dumb, but instead she felt… well, a little underwhelmed.

She was looking at an object with a destructive force capable of leveling a city. This thing, detonated in just the right spot, could kill millions in the blink of an eye. It was a bomb with the capacity to change the course of human history at the push of a button, but now she got a good look at it she realized it was just a plain cylinder of dull gray steel, around two feet long and a foot across. It looked like nothing so much as an old milk churn. A thousand people could walk by it at an antique fair, and none of them would be any the wiser.

"I thought it'd be bigger."

Even as she spoke she was surprised at the hint of disappointment in her own voice. Almost offense, as if it were somehow disrespectful that she might be killed by something so unassuming.

Krasinski leaned over the crate, and despite the worry plastered across his face he managed to flash a grin. "If I had a dollar for every time a woman said that to me…"

"Read the room, Ted," Karen sighed. "This is no time for jokes." She reached into the crate and plucked away a handful of packing material. "Are we absolutely certain this is a nuclear weapon? I thought they were enormous missiles or something."

"Yeah, that's the picture that was in my head. But no, I'm pretty sure this is it. I think this is just the warhead. It's designed to be mounted on the tip of a missile."

"So…" Karen puffed out her cheeks.

"So…?"

"So, do you have any idea how to disarm this thing?"

Krasinski let out a sharp guffaw.

"Seriously?" He ran his fingers through his hair and swore under his breath. "I don't even know if this thing is armed. Do you? All I know about bombs I got from the movies, and unless I see a digital timer with a red and blue wire coming from it I have no clue. And even if I *did* see that stuff there'd be a fifty fifty chance I'd cut the wrong wire and blow all three of us to kingdom come."

"What about that panel there?" Karen pointed towards a steel plate around five by four inches, screwed into the body of the warhead. "Maybe we can unscrew it and take a look inside."

"Do you have a screwdriver handy? *I* don't." Krasinski snapped.

"OK, settle down. I'm just trying to come up with a solution. There's no need to get all pissy."

Krasinski sighed contritely. "Sorry, sorry. You're right. It's just… well, I'd kinda made my peace with dying when I thought there were jets on the way to shoot us down. I knew it was out of my hands, know what I mean? Now, though… well, I guess you could say I'm feeling the pressure." He slumped over the crate, his balding head glistening with sweat.

Karen frowned at the bomb, hoping against hope

that a solution might magically present itself. "OK," she said, pushing herself away from the crate, "let's look at our options here. It's probably safe to say that Bailey plans to use this, right? Whether he plans to land or just drop it from the plane we don't know, but we can be pretty certain he has a target in mind. Agreed?"

Krasinski nodded. "Yeah, that's probably a safe bet."

"OK. If they plan to drop it from the plane then we're dead. There's nowhere to hide if they come back to the truck, and I'm guessing they'd have no problem killing us."

"After dropping nukes on a half dozen cities? No, I'm pretty sure they'd feel comfortable shooting us in the head."

"And if we land we're also dead. You said that cargo bay door won't open when the plane's on the ground, right? While it's moving, anyway?"

"That's right," Krasinski confirmed. "As far as I know it's locked in place while the landing gear are extended, and it won't unlock unless the pilot flips a switch in the cockpit."

"And there's definitely no other way out of here?"

"From the cargo bay? Not with those doors welded

shut, no. One way in, one way out."

Karen felt her heart sink as the realization hit her. She looked down at Emily, oblivious to the danger, quietly humming to herself as she played with a bundle of straw from one of the crates.

"We're going to die, aren't we?"

Krasinski nodded. There didn't seem to be any point denying it.

Karen felt the first warnings of another panic attack coming on. She'd tried to take deep, measured breaths to ward off the fear, but she didn't know a breathing exercise or meditation technique in the world that could win out over the stress of staring down at a nuclear weapon that might go off at any second.

She walked back to the tailgate of the truck, hopped down to the ground and stared at the floor, wishing they'd jumped with Ramos and Valerie. If they'd only had the guts to throw themselves off the back of the truck they could have been walking back towards Beale right now, back towards Jack, instead of being trapped in this damned plane.

She turned back to the truck and leaned on the tailgate. "Come here, pumpkin," she said, holding out her arms for Emily. "Mommy needs a hug."

Emily beamed, grateful for the attention after an eternity of watching the grownups talk about things she didn't understand. She tossed aside the straw, picked herself up and ran to the tailgate, hopping down into her mother's arms. "I don't like it here, mommy. Can we go home?"

"Soon, pumpkin, soon." Karen pulled Emily close, thanking God that she didn't understand what was happening. That was the only silver lining she could see, that when the end came Emily might not notice it. If she was lucky she might–

Karen froze, her eyes fixed on the side wall of the plane. There were only three small windows in the fuselage and the cold blue strip lighting only served to cast a ghostly glow, but in the eerie half light she could see a misshapen lump dangling from a hook on the wall.

"Ted? You said there was a parachute, right?"

"On the wall? Yeah."

"How come there's only one of them?"

Krasinski lowered himself down from the tailgate with a grunt. "There's not. The Hercules crews five. There should be one chute for each of them, but the other four will be up in the cockpit. They keep them close by their stations in case they have to bail out in an emergency." He pointed at the wall. "This one's for the loadmaster. He's the guy who works in the cargo bay during flight."

"Do you think there might be any backups? Y'know, like in a storage locker or something."

"Nuh uh. They don't keep parachutes hidden away. If there were any more here they'd be right there on the wall."

"Damn it," Karen grumbled, walking over to the chute and lifting it from its hook. That put paid to the idea of all three of them leaping out to safety, unless they wanted to take their chances storming the cockpit and overpowering a bunch of highly trained soldiers.

She set Emily down and inspected the pack for damage, running her fingers along the seams for signs of damage. Only God knew how long the chute had been sitting there. The colonel had said this was a decommissioned plane, so this pack could have been hanging from its hook for years without an inspection, ready to fall apart at the lightest touch.

She flipped open the flap, and she was relieved to find it had been packed properly. Karen had done a half dozen jumps back in her twenties, in the brief period before Robbie had come along when she'd tried to convince herself she was a badass adrenaline junkie, but she'd never packed her own chute. She'd have no idea how to do it herself.

She lifted Emily back to her shoulder, turned to the back of the plane and nodded toward the cargo ramp. "Ted, you said that thing wouldn't open when the plane was on the ground, right? How about when we're in the air?"

Krasinski paused before answering, and Karen could see the color draining from his face as he saw the chute dangling from her hand and worked out what she was suggesting. "Well, I mean, yeah, it'll open in flight," he stammered. "There should be a manual release somewhere near the door. You want to jump?"

"No," Karen replied. She shuffled Emily higher on her shoulder, walked back to the truck and held out the chute. "I want *you* to jump."

Krasinski's jaw dropped. "Me?" he stammered. "Why me?"

"Take it." She pushed the chute against his chest. "It's a tandem rig. You can take Emily with you."

Krasinski reluctantly took the chute from her hand, shaking his head. "I don't understand. Why do you want *me* to jump?"

"Because of what's in that envelope, Ted. You need to get the evidence back to the government. You need to stop them from doing something stupid before it's too late, and I can't do it. I wouldn't even know who to call. It has to be you."

Krasinski tried to hand the chute back to Karen, but she pushed it away. "I can't take this. I don't even know how it works!"

"It's simple, Ted," Karen insisted. "See this cord right here?" She grabbed a thin white rope protruding from the top of the pack. "You hook that into the rail. You see it?" She turned and pointed, and Krasinski noticed the rail running along the wall at head height. "The chute deploys on its own as soon as you jump. You don't have to do anything at all. It's completely foolproof."

"No!" Krasinski protested. "Look, this is stupid. I"m not leaving you up here. What kind of a mother would just abandon her daughter like– "

The slap was so hard it almost knocked Ted from his feet. He staggered back against the tailgate, dropping the chute to the ground, and he blinked away the pain as a bright red handprint bloomed on his cheek. "Wha– "

"I'd doing this *because* I'm a mother," Karen

hissed. "I need to keep Emily safe, and not just from this but from whatever the hell comes next. It's no good getting her to the ground only to land her in the middle of a nuclear war. You need to get her back to her daddy, Ted. You need to *promise* me. Get her to Jack Archer, but first you have to deliver that evidence to the people who can stop this. Do you understand me?"

Krasinski looked stunned. "Yeah," he mumbled. "Yeah, I understand." He reached down and reluctantly scooped the chute from the floor. "What are you going to do?"

Karen was already reaching for the first of the ratchet straps that connected the wheels of the truck to the cargo deck. With a sharp tug the strap came loose.

"I'm going to stop them from doing whatever they're planning to do," she said, pulling the strap free of the tire. "I'm going to get rid of this thing before they can set it off."

Krasinski gulped. "You think you're going to just push the truck out the back?"

"No," Karen moved onto the second strap. "As soon as you're clear of the plane I'm going to drive it out."

Krasinski sighed, defeated. He could see the determination in Karen's eyes, and he knew there was no way of changing her mind. "OK. OK, I'll jump. But can you show me how this thing works again? How do I strap Emily in?"

"It's simple." Karen grabbed the chute from his hands, pointing to the harness at the front. "You just tighten it over your shoulders, and when you're securely fastened in you clip her in at the chest right here. See these clips?"

He nodded. "I see them. And the chute's big enough to support our weight?"

"Yeah. It's enough to hold two Marines. Don't worry, you'll be fine."

"OK." Krasinski looked miserable as he stared down at the clips. "Hand Emily over. I'll get her strapped in."

Karen nodded. "OK, pumpkin, you're going to go with Ted now."

Emily squirmed in her arms as she tried to pass her over. "Where are we going?"

Karen smiled, stroking her hair. "Ted's taking you to meet daddy."

"Really?" Emily's eyes lit up. "Are we all going home?"

Karen felt tears well in her eyes. "Yeah, pumpkin, very soon. I just have to do something first, OK?" She squeezed Emily tight. "But listen, I need you to promise me something. I need you to be good for your daddy, OK?"

"I promise, mommy."

"I'm serious. No more fighting at school, OK?"

Emily nodded. "OK, mommy, no more fighting."

"Good girl," she whispered. "Now come here. I want an extra big hug."

Karen held her little girl close, sniffing away a tear. She held the hug as long as she could, trying to commit to memory every detail. The tickle of Emily's hair on her nose. The unfamiliar smell of the shampoo she'd used back at Beale. The soft warmth of her skin against her cheek. The little heartbeat fluttering out of sync with her own.

She wanted *this* to be her last memory. Nothing that came after mattered. When the time came she wanted to remember this. This hug. This feeling. She wanted to know in her final moments that she'd done everything she could to keep her little girl safe. To get her back to her daddy.

"OK, pumpkin," she whispered, her voice trembling as she fought back the tears, "it's time to go."

Karen reluctantly passed her over, holding on until the final moment, and as Krasinski pulled the chute over his shoulder she wiped a tear from her cheek. She couldn't bear to watch. She didn't want to see when he finally took her away.

"I need to get the other straps," she muttered, turning away and rushing to the far side of the truck, and she only just made it out of sight before the tears came in a flood.

Great, silent sobs racked her chest. She refused to let Emily see her cry, but the effort of holding back a mournful wail was almost too much to bear. She had to lean against the truck for support as her legs threatened to give way beneath her.

"Hey, Karen?" Behind her she heard Krasinski's voice, but she couldn't face him, either.

"Just give me a minute, Ted," she pleaded. "I need a second alone."

She leaned both hands flat against the truck, trying to force herself to stop crying, but it was no good. The tears just kept flowing.

"Karen, I'm– "

"*Just a minute*, Ted," she insisted.

"I'm really sorry about this."

She looked up just in time to see the iron pry bar swing.

She didn't feel it hit.

Everything went black.

•▼•

CHAPTER TWENTY

T MINUS 87 SECONDS

"SIR, I HAVE Nellis for you on VHF. Major Strachan is awaiting your order."

MacAuliffe stared at the radar screen on the cockpit's central console. The Hercules was just a few miles ahead of them, almost within sight. He adjusted the mic on his headset and began to speak.

"Major, have you located the C-130?"

Jack heard a crackle in his own headset as the reply came. They were only just within radio range of the base, and the voice in his ears sounded ghostly and distant.

"That's affirmative, sir. We have it on a bearing of one three two degrees at one niner four knots. At current airspeed it'll reach Las Vegas in seventeen minutes. Fifteen until it's over populated areas."

MacAuliffe nodded to himself. "Major, can you confirm missile lock on target?"

Jack held his breath.

"Confirmed, sir. We have a Patriot locked and loaded, ready to fire on your order."

Jack reached out and grabbed MacAuliffe's arm. "Don't do it," he pleaded. "Please, just give them a couple more minutes."

The colonel shrugged his arm away. "I'm sorry, Jack. If they'd managed to pull something off the plane would have changed course by now, but they're still headed straight as an arrow for the city. I've given them all the time I can afford."

"We have seventeen minutes!" Jack insisted. "You can afford to wait a couple more!"

"Do I have the go order, sir?"

Standby, major," MacAuliffe growled, turning back to Jack. "No, son, I don't have seventeen minutes. Right now they're sixty miles from the edge of the city, and every minute we wait they move four miles closer. If we don't launch now… this is our last chance." He shook his head sadly. "I'm sorry."

Jack felt his heart race in his chest. He felt the sudden insane urge to leap forward and grab the controls from the pilot, to send the Chinook into a dive and keep the colonel from giving his order, but he knew it was hopeless. He knew it was always a million to one shot that Karen could somehow take control of the plane and steer it out of danger. He knew he'd been clutching at straws.

"Just one more minute, colonel, *please*," he begged, staring at the radar screen, willing the little green blinking dot to take a sudden turn.

"Fire."

Jack's blood turned to ice in his veins, and a moment later the ice became acid as the voice returned over the radio.

"Missile is away. Intercept in T minus eighty seven seconds."

Out the front windshield of the Chinook the Hercules was finally coming into view. It had slowed on its approach to the city, its speed dipping so low they'd been able to claw back the space between them. Now it was a black dot in the clear blue sky a few miles to the east.

Jack couldn't tear his eyes away from it. He blinked away tears, wishing with all his heart that he could trade places with Karen and Emily. Right now he'd tear it from his chest and throw it at the missiles if it might help throw them off course, but all he could do was sit and watch, waiting for the moment the little black dot exploded, and with it his wife and child.

"T minus sixty seconds to intercept. Course holding."

"You don't want to watch this, Jack," MacAuliffe suggested, patting his shoulder. Jack shrugged him away, his eyes fixed on the plane ahead. They were close enough now that he could make out the wings.

"T minus forty five seconds."

"Seriously, Jack, you don't want this memory." MacAuliffe tried to gently push him away from the cockpit, but Jack pushed back.

"Neither do you, colonel." He could barely see through the tears in his eyes. He clenched his jaw and held firm, watching the plane as the sunlight caught the tail.

"T minus... standby." Over the radio there was a sudden clamor of voices before the major returned. "Colonel, what happened? A second target just appeared on our radar."

MacAuliffe and Jack both leaned forward in their seats, staring intently at the plane in the distance. They were still too far away to make out any details, but there were now two shapes in the sky ahead. The plane continued onward on the same course, but beneath it something large was falling away, fast.

"Oh my God," MacAuliffe breathlessly gasped.

Jack gripped the back of the pilot's seat. "What is it?"

MacAuliffe stared open mouthed at the falling dot, the sun catching its side, dazzling them as it tumbled. He turned to Jack with a grim expression, his face drained of color.

"I think Bailey dropped the bomb."

•▼•

CHAPTER TWENTY ONE
TED KRASINSKI DAY

KRASINSKI SWORE UNDER his breath, clenching his hand into a fist to stop it from trembling.

"Get it together, Ted," he whispered to himself, resting the crumpled manila envelope against the tailgate of the truck as he grabbed the pen once again. The words still came out almost illegible. They crept across the paper like the shaky, uncertain chicken scratch of a lifelong drunk, but it would have to do. There was no time for him to worry about his penmanship.

He knew the clock was against him. He hadn't realized how difficult it would be to get Karen's dead weight strapped in, and he definitely hadn't figured on Emily screaming and fighting back. That particular complication hadn't even occurred to him when he'd come up with his hare-brained plan.

He hated that he had to do it, but when Emily saw him hit her mom over the head she'd screamed bloody murder. He couldn't risk her screams reaching the people in the cockpit so he'd had to spend another couple of minutes gagging the girl with the torn off sleeve of his corduroy jacket, and even more time binding her hands with one of the ratchet straps. It was the only way to shut her up short of knocking her out, and he just couldn't bring himself to do that to a child. Not after he'd felt the sickening thud reverberate down the tire iron as it struck Karen's skull. He could never do *that* again.

Karen had been out cold for five minutes now, but Krasinski knew that she wouldn't stay that way much longer, not with Emily squirming on top of her, trying desperately to free herself. Her muffled yells were still loud enough to wake the dead, though thankfully they were drowned out by the drone of the engines.

"*Please* be quiet, Emily," he pleaded, but he knew it was a fool's errand. Nothing he could say right now would calm her down. After what she'd seen him do to her mom he was a Bad Guy, end of story, and she'd keep screaming until Karen woke up and dealt with him.

Krasinski froze, staring down at the prone body at his feet. Karen muttered something, her lips moving but the words almost silent. She squeezed her eyes tight and curled her lip, wincing as the pain of the blow reached her even through the unconscious fog. He only had a few seconds now. God help him if she woke before he was ready.

Now he felt his heart race in his chest. Even the Xanax he'd tossed back wasn't enough to keep him calm. He felt the panic creeping up on him, and he knew that if he let it overwhelm him all of this would be for nothing. He needed to hold on just a little longer. He took a deep, slow breath, forcing the panic into the background.

Timing was everything. The moment the cargo door began to open he knew an alarm would sound in the cockpit. The plane would depressurize. It would be chaos, and he'd only have a few seconds before someone would back from the cockpit, armed and ready to fire. But he *also* knew they'd hear him in the cockpit if he fired up the engine of the truck. Either way he'd only have seconds to spare, and there was no way he could deal with Karen at the same time. There was just no way.

This isn't going to work.

He swore again, louder this time, and he stalked around to the side of the truck and slipped his arms beneath Karen. She was heavier than he expected, especially with Emily's wriggling, uncooperative weight attached to her, but the adrenaline gave him just enough strength to lift her from the ground. With a grunt he hefted her up to the passenger seat of the truck, dropping her in place like a rag doll and stuffing her legs in after her. She grunted, mumbling again, but he didn't have time to worry about her waking. He only had seconds now.

He grabbed hold of the cord from the parachute pack, tying it off around the steering wheel of the truck, and then he ran back to the top of the cargo ramp, searching the wall until he found the control panel. The enormous red button jumped out at him, large enough to be slapped with a gloved hand, and with a silent prayer he punched at it with his fist.

Nothing happened.

He slapped it again, pushing it until he felt firm resistance, but again nothing happened.

"What the hell?"

He couldn't believe this was happening. All this fear, all this risk, and it was all for nothing if he couldn't open the damned cargo door. If he couldn't open the door he'd be back where he started, staring death in the face, but now he'd have to go through it with Karen hating him and Emily fearing him. He'd have to–

Wait.

Just below the red button was a switch, a rubberized black toggle with the words RAMP LOCK etched in white. He flipped the switch, and immediately a deafening klaxon began to sound through the cargo bay. A blinking yellow light began to flash on and off above the control panel, and when he slapped the button again the light turned to red.

The door began to open.

The sudden rush of air as the bay depressurized threatened to knock Krasinski off his feet. He grabbed hold of the edge of the control panel, steadying himself against the gale, and his heart leaped to his throat as he caught a glimpse of clear blue sky out the back of the plane. He gripped the panel tighter as the ramp completed its descent with a loud mechanical bang, holding on for dear life even after the gale died down. He knew he was perfectly safe where he was standing. He was just as safe as he'd been when the ramp was closed, but now he knew that if he took two steps to his right he'd be on the ramp, and after the steel grating ended there was nothing beyond but twenty thousand feet of clear air.

Krasinski shivered, turning back to the truck as he forced himself to let go of the control panel and make his way on unsteady legs back to the cab. He could barely take a breath in the thin air, gasping for a lungful that felt empty of oxygen, but he didn't let it stop him. Nothing could keep him from climbing behind the wheel now.

"Ted?"

He froze. Karen was awake in the passenger seat, only half conscious but present enough to notice her daughter pressed against her chest, her hands bound and a length of tan corduroy strapped across her mouth. "What are you doing?" she slurred. "What's going on?"

"I…" he began to answer, but he was interrupted by a sudden shower of sparks exploding against the driver's door. For a split second he stared at the door, confused, before a second gunshot punched through the windshield, shattering it into a cobweb of glistening edges.

"Get down!" he yelled, throwing himself into the driver's seat and fumbling for the key. The shooter was ahead them, holding onto the rail of a gantry that led towards the cockpit, in a perfect position to hit them unless they pressed flat against the seats. As his hand found the key hanging from the ignition Krasinski reached out and grabbed Karen's shoulder with the other, dragging the dazed woman down below the base of the windshield, out of sight of the shooter.

"Ted, what's happening?" Karen demanded, looking down at the straps tied across her body.

Krasinski ignored her. With a grunt of effort he shifted the truck into reverse gear, and he reached blindly into the footwell and pressed his hand against the gas pedal.

Another shot showered them in glass shards as the windshield gave out, and Krasinski released the gas as he flinched with shock, reaching up to protect his head from the glass that rained down over them. The truck slowed, but it didn't stop. It kept creeping backwards even as their attacker emptied his magazine into the engine.

Krasinski moved on instinct. If he took the time to think he knew he'd freeze, so instead he lunged across

Karen's body, pulled the door handle and pushed it open as the truck reached the edge of the descending ramp. They were moving at a crawl now, slower than walking pace, but it was enough. With a loud thunk the rear wheels dropped off the edge of the ramp, and as it continued to descend Krasinski reached down and pressed hard on the gas, launching the truck back with a jolt before it ground to a halt, teetering on the ramp's edge. For a moment it hung there, ignored by gravity, perfectly balanced on the sliver of steel.

And then it fell.

Krasinski grabbed hold of the wheel as his stomach flipped over. The back of the truck tipped out over clear air, so slowly that he feared it might tilt back to the other way, but after a moment of indecision gravity finally set its course. The truck fell backwards, its underside grinding along the ramp, and with a final bump the front tires bounced off the edge and out into space.

"*Ted!*" Karen's eyes were wide now. She was fully awake, and Emily's muffled, terrified screams rang through the cab.

"I'm sorry!" he yelled, dragging himself back into his seat. "It's the only way!" He pressed his back against the driver's door, eyes bulging with fear, and with all his strength he braced his feet against Karen's side and pushed, straightening his legs.

Karen screamed. She tried to fight back, to grab hold of something, anything to hold her steady, but Ted was determined. He kicked out at her hands as she tried to clutch the dash, and with a final violent kick he sent her and Emily tumbling out the passenger door and into open air.

He could still hear her scream as the cord pulled taut against the steering wheel. With a sharp tug it broke free from the pack, and as the truck continued to fall he looked up through the shattered windshield and saw the canopy billow open, Karen and Emily suspended beneath it.

The roar of the wind seemed to fade, and the fear seemed to drift away. It was over now, he knew. There was nothing more to be done. Just a few more seconds.

Karen's chute drifted gracefully through the air above him, green silk against a clear blue sky. Far above the canopy the Hercules lumbered on, the hulking, bulbous cargo plane forging towards a target Krasinski knew was now safe.

Bailey couldn't hurt anyone else. He'd failed, and soon enough everyone would know what he'd done.

Krasinski closed his eyes, waiting for the final moment to come, but a moment later they snapped open at the sound of a roar so loud it beat the wind passing by the truck.

Above him a missile screamed through the sky, impossibly fast, trailing behind it a white contrail that looked like a kite string against the blue. A moment later it met its target, and Krasinski watched open mouthed as the Hercules vanished in a billow of golden fire.

He closed his eyes once more, and a grin flickered across his lips as he whispered his final words.

"Ted Krasinski Day."

He was still smiling as the truck hit the ground.

•▼•

CHAPTER TWENTY TWO
LIKE A PIG ON A SPIT

EVERYONE IN THE Chinook held their breath as they watched the black dot fall away from the Hercules.

Everyone but Jack. Jack didn't care if a nuke was plummeting towards the ground. He wouldn't care if the mushroom cloud engulfed him, if the fireball vaporized him, or the entire world. None of it mattered any more. If it was a world without Karen and his little girl, what was the point in it?

He closed his eyes, waiting for the voice on the radio to confirm that the missile had reached its target.

"T minus five seconds... four... three... two... one... intercept."

Jack felt numb. The steady thump of the rotors faded into the background, and around him the chatter of the pilot turned to white noise. MacAuliffe ordered the Chinook to turn north, to clear the area in case the bomb detonated on impact, but Jack didn't give a damn.

"Target destroyed. Repeat, target destroyed. Do you have visual confirmation?"

MacAuliffe spoke into his headset. "Confirmed, major. Good job."

Good job.

His family was gone, snatched away when they were almost in arm's reach, and it was a *good job*. Jack felt rage and disgust swell in his chest. At MacAuliffe. At General Bailey. At the people at Nellis who'd pushed the launch button.

But most of all he felt disgusted at himself. It seemed like a thousand years ago now, but it had only been this morning that he'd awoken in a comfortable motel bed. It had only been half a day since he'd taken a hot shower, padded across to the sheriff's house and loaded down his plate with pancakes and bacon, relaxing over breakfast, convincing himself that an extra hour or two couldn't possibly matter.

I could have saved them.

He could have kept driving through the night. He could have forced the sheriff to open the gas station, at gunpoint if necessary. He could have done a hundred things differently that might have shaved a little time off his journey, but instead he'd taken his sweet God damn time over breakfast and told himself that he could make it up on the road. And now his wife and daughter were–

"*Open chute!* Sir, I have an open chute in the air!"

"What?" Jack's eyes snapped open and he leaned into the cockpit, staring out the front window. "Where?"

"Two o'clock." The co-pilot pointed to a spot a couple thousand feet beneath the smudge of black on the sky that was all that remained of the Hercules. "Green canopy, just above the horizon."

"What the hell's going on here?" MacAuliffe demanded. The large object that had fallen from the Hercules was still a few thousand feet in the air, still plummeting to the ground, but the parachute seemed to be slowly descending directly above it. "Hold this position," MacAuliffe ordered, "and keep your eye on that damned chute. If that's Bailey I'll be damned if we're letting him get away."

"Yes, sir," the co-pilot confirmed. "The…

ummm… the bomb is at two thousand feet, sir."

Jack craned over the pilot's seat to watch as the object neared the ground. If that really was Bailey hanging beneath the chute he wanted to see the fireball engulf him. He wanted to watch that bastard die like a pig on a spit, suspended above the fire he'd created.

"Twelve hundred… eight hundred… four hundred… brace for turbulence."

Jack squinted his eyes, ready to turn away when the flash came, but there was nothing. At this distance the impact was barely even visible. The falling object simply vanished, kicking up a cloud of dust as it hit the barren ground.

"Negative detonation, sir."

MacAuliffe frowned, staring at the distant puff drifting away on the breeze. It was obvious he'd been expecting an explosion, and now he didn't seem to know what to do. "OK, hold position for five minutes before approaching. I don't want to get caught in the blast if it's in laydown mode." He turned to Jack, patting him on the shoulder. "We're gonna get that bastard, don't you worry. If that's Bailey in the air you can look him in the eye before we take him in."

Jack nodded, staring at the chute as it drifted slowly across the clear blue sky. If that *was* Bailey he wanted to do more than look him in the eye. That wouldn't be nearly enough. He couldn't just watch the man who'd killed his wife and daughter get a set of handcuffs slapped on his wrists.

He had to kill him.

•▼•

CHAPTER TWENTY THREE

SPECIAL DELIVERY

KAREN LET OUT a piercing scream as Krasinski kicked at her, pushing her inch by inch from the truck and into the clear air. She was still only half awake, confused and terrified, and she had no idea what was going on. No idea why he was doing this, or why Emily was bound and gagged, strapped to her chest. None of it made sense to her. All she knew – all she *thought* she knew – was that for some reason Krasinski was trying to kill her, and her only option was to fight back.

But it was no use. She clawed at his legs and tried to grab hold of anything within reach, but he was too determined. He kicked out at her without mercy, crushing her fingers with the heel of his shoe when she managed to get purchase on part of the truck. She fought desperately to keep herself inside the truck, but it wasn't long before the fight was lost. Her crushed fingers reached out and found nothing more to grab.

The wind caught her as her body edged out through the door, and she found herself staring down at the ground thousands of feet below, a disorienting sight seen through tear filled eyes. With a final violent shove her legs slipped from the truck and she tumbled into the sky. She tried to twist in mid air. She frantically screamed as she turned and reached out, making one last grab at the door frame, but her fingertips only brushed against it as she fell away.

And then… then she felt a sharp tug at her back. She tried to get a look at what was happening, but all she could see was a white rope spooling out behind her, an umbilical cord connecting her to the truck as it drifted further away with every second. She reached out to grab it, hoping to pull herself back in, but the moment her first wrapped around the cord it pulled taut with a snap, and she jerked forward so violently it felt as if she'd been kicked in the neck.

With a billowing *whumph* the parachute whipped out above her, and before she knew what was happening she felt her fall suddenly arrested. Her head sunk to her chest, and Emily hung like a rag doll in front of her as the chute yanked them from gravity's embrace.

'*Ngh!*'

The air was squeezed from her lungs as the straps of the chute cut into her chest, and in the thin air she struggled to find her breath. She was in agony as she gasped for air, but finally she understood what was happening. Finally she understood that Ted was trying to *save* her, not hurt her.

With numb fingers she pried at the knot he'd tied in Emily's gag, and when it came away she shied away from the piercing scream.

"It's alright, pumpkin," she gasped, trying and failing to keep her voice calm. "We're safe now. We'll be on the ground soon."

Emily squirmed in her straps, screaming and struggling as if she might somehow be able to escape, and for a moment Karen was filled with dread. What if Ted hadn't clipped them in right? What if Emily's wriggling sent her slipping out of the pack, tumbling to the ground far below?

She grabbed her daughter around the waist and held tight, so tight that she couldn't scream any longer, and with her free hand she ran her fingers across the thick black straps until she found the heavy duty steel clips. With a relieved sigh she pulled on the clips and found they were securely fastened.

Emily gasped for air when Karen finally released her vice-like grip, crying with pain, her ribs squeezed almost to breaking point.

"I'm so sorry, pumpkin," she said. "I didn't mean to hurt you but– "

Her voice was drowned out by a roar above them. Her head snapped up, but the green silk obscured half the sky. All she could see was an orange glow through the canopy, almost as bright as a second sun, and for a moment she was confused.

We took the nuke off the plane. How is it exploding above us?

The answer came a moment later. Trailing thick black smoke the nose of the Hercules broke past the edge of the chute. It arced down towards the ground, tumbling end on end as a fragment of wing followed it, its twin rotors still spinning uselessly.

Karen braced herself, shielding Emily with her arms as the debris showered down from the sky above. She was certain they'd be hit. The sky seemed to be so filled with steel rain that it was only a matter of time before some of it would tear through the canopy. She gripped hold of the straps at her shoulders and clenched her teeth, waiting for the telltale flapping sound that would tell her the canopy had been holed, but it didn't come. All around them the debris fell, but somehow the chute remained intact.

Emily tried to turn around in her harness, panicked. "Mommy, what's happening?"

"I'm right here pumpkin," Karen soothed, wrapping her arms around her daughter. "I'm right here, and we're safe." She looked down at the ground just as the truck reached it, and from above she saw nothing but a puff of dust. "Ted saved us."

She looked up at the suspension lines above her, and with a stretch she reached for the control lines and sent the chute into a swoop to the left. She didn't know if the nuke could survive an impact like that without damage, but the last thing she wanted to do was come down anywhere near the truck. With another gentle tug of a line she straightened up, sending them in a glide with the wind toward the south.

Something was poking Karen's chest, somewhere beneath the straps of the chute. Emily's wriggling seemed to have dislodged it, and now it shifted further up until a sharp edge pricked at her throat. She reached beneath the straps and carefully plucked it out.

It was Krasinski's envelope. She tightened her grip on it, terrified of letting it float away, and she flipped it over to find a passage scrawled on the back.

Karen, get this to Maj. Gen. Holden, Nellis AFB. Tell him to forward it to the Joint Chiefs right away. On page four you'll find the accounts for Parris Island. They'll find the link to Gen. Bailey if they dig deep enough.

Good luck. Try to make sure the news runs an old picture of me with a full head of hair.

Karen smiled, tucking the envelope tight between her chest and the harness, where there was no danger of the wind snatching it away.

The ground was coming up fast now, rocky and rough in burnt orange and gray. She grabbed hold of the brake lines and pulled, tugging the rear of the chute down and sending them into a slow glide to the ground.

She'd never made a tandem jump before. She knew she wouldn't be able to keep to her feet with Emily's weight pulling her forward, and she knew it would be especially difficult now that her daughter had noticed the ground approaching. She wriggled in her harness, shrieking with fear as the ground rushed past beneath them, and Karen realized she had no choice but to take the hit.

She lifted her legs, and with a final sharp tug on the brake lines she felt her butt hit the ground, bouncing on the hard earth and taking the speed out of their glide. Emily's legs rested in Karen's lap as she hit the ground again, this time scraping along a rocky patch, but this time she didn't bounce back into the air. The chute collapsed around them as they rolled over and over, binding them up in the lines and shrouding them in darkness.

Finally they came to rest, battered and bruised but alive. Karen lay on her side, her arms wrapped protectively around her daughter, and for a moment she held her breath, waiting for the pain to announce itself.

"Are we... are we on the ground?" Emily's disembodied voice meekly called out through the canopy.

Karen took a hesitant breath. She couldn't feel any broken bones. A few inches of road rash on her ass, maybe, but nothing that would stop her walking out of there.

"Yes, pumpkin," she replied, breaking into a laugh as she unclipped Emily from the harness. "We're on the ground."

Emily sniffed.

"Can... can we *stay* on the ground?"

●▼●

CHAPTER TWENTY FOUR
CAN WE GO HOME NOW?

JACK WAS THE first out of the Chinook, running ahead of MacAuliffe as soon as the door opened. He heard the colonel yelling behind him, warning him to stop, but he ignored the order. He didn't owe the man anything.

The green silk caught in the breeze, billowing out loosely from a body bound up beneath it, and as he approached he could see that whoever was in there was struggling to fight their way free. Jack felt his fists bunch, preparing himself for what came next. He guessed that even a Marine close to retirement would be able to beat him in a fair fight, and he knew he'd have to take the general by surprise if he hoped to take him down.

He slowed as he approached the canopy, ready to launch himself at whatever came out, and he was so focused on it that he was taken completely by surprise when MacAuliffe appeared out of nowhere and tackled him to the ground.

"*No!*" yelled the colonel. "We do this by the book, damn it!"

Jack swore at him, his face caked in dust where his cheek pressed against the ground. MacAuliffe drew his pistol and held it aloft in his free hand, pinning Jack with the other, and they both watched and waited as the struggling figure reached the edge of the silk.

The wind caught it, and with a sudden gust the figure was revealed.

"Karen?" He felt MacAuliffe's weight vanish from above him, and he pulled himself to his knees. He couldn't believe what he was seeing "*Karen!*"

She looked dazed, limping out from beneath the canopy, her eyes casting about, but her attention snapped to the sound of her name.

"Jack?" she mumbled, disbelieving the evidence of her eyes. "How… how are you…?"

Jack didn't wait to answer. He bolted from the ground like a sprinter, covering the distance between them in the blink of an eye, and he took Karen in his arms with the desperation and gratitude of a man rescued after years trapped on a desert island. He held her tight even as the chute caught the wind and tried to pull them off their feet, and he only let go when he felt an insistent tug at his leg.

"Daddy?"

Jack looked down, and his heart melted at the sight of his little girl, her hair windswept and her grubby cheeks streaked with tears. He swept her from her feet, and she clung onto him so tight it hurt. He didn't care. He'd never let her go again.

"We were in an airplane, daddy," Emily said, her voice muffled as she buried her face in his chest, "but we fell out."

"I saw it, pumpkin," Jack smiled. "I watched you float all the way down."

Emily pulled away and shook her head, her eyes wide. "I didn't like it. Daddy. Can we go home now?"

Jack nodded firmly, sniffing away a tear, and he gave Karen a hopeful look. "Yeah, I think we should all go home."

Karen shook her head, and Jack's heart sank. For a moment he thought she'd pull Emily away. He thought maybe he'd misunderstood. Maybe she didn't want him back after all, but then she spoke. "We can't go home yet. It's not over."

"It is," Jack assured her. "It's OK, they shot down the plane. There are no more bombs."

"No," Karen insisted. "That's not what I mean." She looked over Jack's shoulder at the colonel, narrowing her eyes. "Do you trust him?" she whispered, leaning in to Jack's shoulder.

"What? Trust who?"

"The guy behind you. Can we trust him?"

Jack nodded without hesitation. He'd never forgive MacAuliffe for ordering the missile strike, but he'd trust him to the ends of the earth. "Yeah, we can. Why?"

Karen pulled away, reached beneath her harness and slipped out the envelope. "Because," she said, "there's one more thing we have to do. *Then* we can go home."

•▼•

CHAPTER TWENTY FIVE
WEATHER, THEN SPORTS

BEALE AIR FORCE Base hummed with activity. Just a few hours earlier it had been almost deserted, a skeleton staff keeping the lights on while everyone else decamped to the safe zone, but now...

Tens of thousands of survivors milled around outside the administration building and vehicle bay, hiding in whatever shade they could find while volunteers and enlisted men wheeled out a seemingly endless supply of water bottles and MREs. Hundreds more refugees had been crowded into the base housing, mostly children, the elderly and the injured, shielded from the searing California sun.

Every few minutes the roar of a newly arrived cargo plane droned overhead, and soldiers and airmen ran back and forth like workers in an ant colony, each of them on a desperately important assignment that gave them license to shove their way rudely through the crowds.

Jack, Karen and Emily sat in a corner of the mess hall, where they jealously guarded the few square feet they'd managed to grab as hundreds of civilians crowded in. They'd been dumped there by MacAuliffe the moment they'd returned from Nellis in the Chinook, and – for now, at least – it seemed they were surplus to requirements. From the moment Karen had handed over the envelope to the major general they'd been demoted to bit players in the drama. Nobody bothered to keep them up to date after that, and when the Chinook was refueled and ready to return they'd been bundled aboard like so much ballast.

Jack didn't care. He had everything he needed right there in the mess hall. As far as he was concerned the world could go hang as long as he kept hold of his little patch of real estate, and as long as Karen and Emily were in it. He leaned against the wall, his arm draped over Karen's shoulder, and he listened with a blissful smile as Emily excitedly brought him up to date on everything that had happened to her over the past couple of days.

He couldn't even begin to keep up with the story. There was news of a scary man in a tunnel who squeezed her too tight, and another scary man with a baseball bat. Doctor Ramos was a big kid who liked fast cars, but mommy was the real racing driver. The way Emily told it she'd launched a car all the way across the Bay Bridge as it collapsed around them. Jack raised a doubtful eyebrow.

"I'll tell you later," Karen laughed, shaking her head.

"And then we went in the helicopter!" Karen squealed, imitating the sound of the rotors. "But then there was this big flash and the driver shouted for us all to hold on tight and we all started going round and round until I felt like I was gonna get sick, but I didn't, and then the helicopter hit the floor and we all had to jump out real quick." Emily took her first breath for what seemed like five minutes. "Daddy, do you like my thing?" She grabbed hold of her red tie. "The bus driver lady gave it to me."

"It's beautiful, pumpkin. Now, how about we– "

"But that was before she jumped out of the thing with Doctor Ramos, and she rolled and rolled on the floor until she– "

"Hey, pumpkin?" Jack interrupted, grabbing her around the waist and pulling her to the ground between him and Karen. "How about we save the rest of the story for later, huh? I think we all need to get a little rest, OK?"

"But daddy," she complained, "I haven't told you about the airplane yet!"

"OK," he laughed, admitting defeat. "Why don't you tell us all about the airplane?"

Before she had the chance to start speaking again, Karen leaped to her feet with a yelp. At the entrance to the mess a familiar figure stepped in, limping on a fresh cast and a pair of crutches.

"Doc!" Karen jumped up and waved in the air until Ramos noticed her, and as Valerie appeared behind him he powered through the crowds, pushing aside stray legs that got in the way of his crutches.

"Coming through, folks. Move it or lose it." When he finally reached the far corner he braced himself for Karen's hug, splaying out his crutches to avoid falling over. "Told you I'd take care of them, Jack," he grinned, before the smile faltered a little. "Well, until I fell out of the truck, anyway."

Jack pulled himself to his feet and slapped Ramos on the back. "Close enough, Ram," he laughed.

"Close enough."

"That was my fault." Beside Ramos Valerie grinned sheepishly, cradling her arm in a sling. "Sorry about that. Cesar just can't help himself when he sees me in trouble." She reached over and hugged Karen with her good arm. "Hey, it's Jack, right?"

Jack nodded as Emily tugged at his leg. "It's the bus driver lady, daddy."

Valerie smiled down at the little girl, and then back to Jack. "There's a guy out in the hallway yelling your name. British guy, kinda snooty. Anyone you know?"

"Doug!" Jack scanned around the canteen, hoping to see him, but there was no sign. He looked at the thronged crowd between him and the door, and rather than force his way through he cupped his hands around his mouth and yelled at the top of his voice.

"Doug! Douglas Garside!"

The mess hall fell silent as everyone turned to stare, but Jack didn't give a damn. A broad smile crept to his lips at the sound of an echoing bark, and a moment later Boomer came bounding through the door and made a beeline for Jack, racing through a forest of legs as Garside struggled to catch up.

"Boomer!" Jack dropped into a crouch and braced himself as the dog leaped excitedly into his arms. "I'm so glad to see you, girl."

Boomer slobbered cheerfully over Jack as Emily's eyes lit up with excitement. "She's just like Custard!" she squealed, wrapping her arms around the hyperactive dog.

"Custard?"

"My mom's new dog," Karen explained. "Emily's crazy for him."

"Ah," Jack nodded. He tilted his head and gave Karen a look, silently posing a question in the language that develops between husband and wife over many years.

Can we keep her?

Karen thought about it for a moment, raised an eyebrow, and then nodded with a smile.

Garside finally pushed his way through the mass of people, stumbling out beside Ramos with a flustered look and pink cheeks. "Good Lord, it's like Waitrose on Christmas Eve in here."

Jack grinned, stepped over Boomer and grabbed Garside in a bear hug. "Good to see you again, old man."

Garside stiffly returned the hug, patting Jack once

on the back before pulling away with an embarrassed expression. "Just a flying visit," he said. "Cathy and I have been searching high and low for you. I wanted to catch you before I leave."

"You're leaving?"

Garside pushed his glasses up the bridge of his nose and smiled. "Yes, there's a plane leaving for somewhere called Barstow in about twenty minutes. Apparently there's a refugee camp down there, and according to the pilot who just flew from there there's a furious English woman with very bad sunburn complaining about the accommodation."

It took Jack a moment to make the connection. "Brenda? They found Brenda?"

Garside grinned and nodded. "Nobody complains like my Brenda. She'll be running the place by the time I get there." He chuckled and lowered himself to a knee, taking Boomer by the collar. "It was nice getting to know you, girl," he said, ruffling the chubby folds of her neck. "Thanks for keeping me company."

Boomer licked Garside's face, and Emily leaned in shyly.

"I really like your dog, mister."

Garside looked up with surprise, and before he

answered he looked up at Jack. "Well, actually," he said, brushing dander from his jacket, "I believe she's *your* dog."

Emily's eyes grew wide as saucers. "Really? Is it true, daddy?"

Jack nodded, grinning. "Well, she's yours if you want her."

"Yes!" Emily yelled out without a pause. "I love her so much!" She threw her arms around the chocolate lab, nuzzling her neck as Boomer basked in the attention.

"I must say," Garside sighed, ruffling Boomer's fur, "I'll miss her when I'm gone."

"Maybe you and Brenda can get a dog of your own when you get home," Jack suggested. "And you're more than welcome to drop in for a visit any time you want to catch up with Boomer." Jack was just being polite, but as he spoke he realized he really *would* welcome a visit. Somehow the cranky, irascible Brit had gotten under his skin on the road from Oregon.

"I might just take you up on that, Jack," Garside smiled. "I'm afraid I've grown rather attached. Well, I'll see you when I see you, Boomer." With a final scratch behind her ear he reluctantly pushed himself to his feet, and he turned away embarrassed when Jack noticed his eyes welling. "Little dusty in here," he muttered, coughing awkwardly as he blinked away the tears.

Jack nodded and gave him a knowing smile. "Yeah, that dust'll get you, Doug."

Garside laughed, wiping his eyes with the back of his hand, and when he caught a flicker high on the wall he welcomed the distraction. A TV screen that had been broadcasting static suddenly resolved into an image.

"Oh, looks like they got the TV signal back."

As soon as he saw it Jack stepped over Boomer, stretched up and cranked up the volume. "Hey, everyone! Quiet! The news is on."

On screen a polished, glossy haired anchorman in a sharp suit looked flustered and red faced as he held his hand to his ear. The crowd in the mess fell silent as his voice rang out.

"… breaking now. We don't have all the details yet, but in a stunning development we hear that new evidence received by the White House suggests that the attacks may have been an act of domestic terrorism, and *not* as previously reported a strike by a foreign power. We're getting…" He looked off screen.

"Phil, do we have a shot?" In the corner of the screen a photograph of a military man appeared, gray haired and decked out with an array of medals on his chest.

"We're getting word that Brigadier General Harlan Thomas Bailey, a Marine Corps officer who until recently was posted at Parris Island, South Carolina, was killed today in an apparent military strike over the skies of Nevada. This is still coming in as we report, but it's believed that General Bailey has connections to the Year Zero group, an extremist organization that authorities now suggest may be linked to a previously unreported 2016 theft of nuclear weapons from a military base overseas."

A murmur passed through the crowd as the anchorman continued.

"Sources at the Pentagon tell us that following a covert military operation in the skies west of Las Vegas the President has ordered the armed forces to stand down from DEFCON 1, and contact has been made with world leaders to assure them that there are no plans to launch retaliatory attacks."

Jack sighed, feeling the stress flow from his body as the anchor continued to speak. He looked at Karen and found her smiling.

"We did it," she whispered, a tear rolling down her

cheek. "It's over."

Jack nodded, pulling her in and holding her close. All around them the crowd of refugees stared up at the screen, transfixed.

"We'll be following this story as it comes in," the anchor went on, "and I'm sure there will be plenty of developments throughout the coming days and weeks. You can stay with CNN for all the breaking updates as the day goes on, and we'll be bringing you the President's address live in about an hour, but for now we'll go to Connie with the weather, and then Todd with sports."

The anchorman flashed a dazzling smile into the camera. "Connie?"

THE END

Thank you for reading *Year Zero*, the final novel in the Jack Archer post-apocalyptic survival trilogy. I hope you enjoyed reading it as much as I enjoyed writing it.

Before you move on (I hope) to my next novel I'd really appreciate it if you'd take a moment to post a review of this book on Amazon. Authors live on caffeine and reviews, and while I'm all set for coffee I have to rely on my readers for the rest.

P.S. If I've ever blown up your home town in one of my stories I'm very sorry. If I've ever *not* blown up your home town in one of my stories I take requests.

Be the first to hear about new releases and sales:
authorkeithtaylor.com/mailing-list/

Contact Keith Taylor directly:
authorkeithtaylor.com
facebook.com/keithtaylorauthor

Printed in Great Britain
by Amazon